# Soul Proprietorship

## Women In Search Of Their Souls

### Dianalee Velie

Plain View Press
P.O. 42255
Austin, TX 78704

plainviewpress.net
sb@plainviewpress.net
512-441-2452

ISBN: 978-1-935514-73-2
Library of Congress Number: 2010938009

Cover art: Sharing Food, watercolour on paper, 14" x 18",  © Melinda Camber Porter.

Cover design by Susan Bright.

Books by Dianalee Velie:
*Glass House*, 2004,
*First Edition*, 2005
*The Many Roads to Paradise*, 2006

# Contents

# Acknowledgments

Grateful acknowledgment to the publications in which these stories have appeared and or won awards

| | |
|---|---|
| *A Christmas Collection* | "Angel's Choice" |
| *A Kiss Is Still a Kiss* | "The Secret Season" |
| *Children, Churches, & Daddies* | "Silent Night" |
| | "Wake Me to Sleep" |
| *Inspirit* | "Five O'clock World" |
| *Hart/A Tome for the Arts* | "Hitchin' a Ride" |
| | "The Baby Born in 1944" |
| *Kalliope* | "Sunflower" |
| *Moon Dance Film Festival/Finalist* | "Boys Will Be Boys" |
| *Moon Dance Film Festival/Semi Finalist* | "Cookie" |
| *Mother of the Groom* | "Mama Says" |
| *New Voices in Poetry and Prose* | "And On the Third Day" |
| *Northwoods Journal* | "Seeking Solitude" |
| *Paws and Tales* | "Hitchin' a Ride" |
| *Potomac Review* | "A Seasonal Education" |
| *Sensations Magazine* | "Five O'clock World" |
| | "Hitchin' a Ride" |
| | "Journey to the Garden of the Waning Moon" |
| | "The Seed" |
| | "Vegetable Fajitas at Vinney's Bar & Grill" |
| *The Ghost in the Gazebo* | "The Family Jewel" |
| *Visions* | "Angel's Choice" |
| *Woman Power* | "A Seasonal Education" |

This book is dedicated to all the beautiful women
who have touched my life
with their dignity, perseverance, bravery and love.


*With stammering lips and insufficient sounds*
*I strive and struggle to deliver right the music of my nature.*

Elizabeth Barrett Browning

# The Secret Season

"A desire fulfilled is sweet to the soul."
Proverbs 13:19

Marci's attention was elsewhere. It was hard going back home after all these years. Harder still when she remembered why she had left. That year, her first year at college, away from home, her parents had chosen to separate. The ensuing divorce ripped at the core of their family like an unleashed tornado weaving its own path of destruction. Within that single year, Marci's dad was dead of a heart attack, leaving her no time to work out the combination of hate and love she felt for him. She swore she would never marry and be dependent on any man or devastated by his infidelities the way her mom had been. It had taken her mother years to rebuild her life. Neither woman would ever be the same. So it surprised her now, sitting in the front seat of the car with Greg, that first of all, she had decided to accept his marriage proposal and, to her own shock, consented to be married in her hometown.

The austere rock ledges towered, buttressing the roadway, heralding her arrival home. It always amazed her, driving into the valley, how the highway slashed open the mountains, exposing these slates of dark brown granite. With the ice cascading down their sides, the stones reminded her of the iced gingerbread cakes her mom used to bake on cold winter days like today when the sky ached clear blue and tiny cotton-y coverlets of clouds floated in the frigid air. Marci was gazing out the window at the snow-covered countryside when they passed the Meadow Sweet Herb Farm.

"I worked there for a summer, Greg. I don't think I ever told you." Marci smiled as she kept her eyes on the passing landscape. She had told him so much about her childhood and the sharp betrayal of her parents' divorce, but never about that summer with Angela. "What a strange season. She was so special." Marci said, more to herself than to Greg.

"Who was?" Greg answered, turning to see Marci still absorbed in the scenery.

"Angela. Angela was my best friend back then. I've never told you about my summer on the farm." Marci almost whispered, smiling sadly to herself. Would it change things if she told Greg, told him everything?

Greg drove on, so happy and absorbed with their upcoming wedding, it took him a few moments to notice the sudden change in Marci's voice.

"You got so quiet. Are you getting nervous? This next stop should be a simple one," he rattled on. "Maybe you can carry fresh herbs in your wedding bouquet." He turned and saw her still staring out the car window long after they'd passed the farm. "Are you OK, sweetie, or is all this running around catching up with you?" he asked, reaching over to touch her shoulder.

Marci turned to look at Greg. She really did love him, but could he ever understand? Angela had been right. She told Marci one day she would marry and have a family, but she was wrong when she said she would soon forget her. Seven years had come and gone since the summer of her nineteenth birthday and the memory of Angela remained as vivid as the brilliant summer flowers they had picked and dried together. Marci returned to college in the fall, more mature, ready to embrace new passages in her life. Just as Angela had predicted, after a few months of correspondence, their letters to each other became sporadic, then ceased.

"The seasons change," Angela had mused in her last letter, the one Marci never answered, "and giving in to nature, so do we."

At last she spoke. "I learned so much that summer, Greg. I learned how to dry and preserve flowers and grasses and seeds and turn them into lasting treasures. I learned how to operate the kiln and to . . . well, to be one with myself. Such an idyllic lifestyle, operating the kiln all winter and growing herbs and flowers in the summer, I thought I wanted to spend the rest of my life right there with her."

"We're here, sweetheart. Let's see what kind of flowers you'll pick for your bouquet." Greg planted a kiss on her cheek, oblivious to her musings, and they both entered the local floral shop.

"So this is the lucky man we've all been hearing about." The proprietors of the shop had known Marci since she was a little girl. It was comfortable introducing them to Greg. He was the kind of guy everyone seemed to like at first glance. She squeezed his hand even tighter and smiled as they began pouring over photo albums filled with various bridal flower arrangements.

"Mrs. Hill, I've been thinking that I'd like to carry a dried flower arrangement, you know a Tussy Mussie. I used to make them myself that summer I worked at the farm." Marci got up and walked to the window. "Greg, we should take a walk up to the farm. I'd like to tell you all about my summer there, my summer with Angela."

"Now she was a weird one," Mrs. Hill began, eager to regain their attention. "You know she never mixed with the people in this town. Lived here for ten years and then just upped and left. Marci probably knew her better than anyone else. You couldn't drag her away from the farm that summer. Why, they did everything together. People were begi...." She stopped herself abruptly, then paused. "Oh well, that was a long time ago. I think that a Tussy Mussie would be really appropriate," Mrs. Hill said, getting back to the flowers. "Here, let me show you the dried flowers I have in stock. You know, no one ever bought her farm," she said as an after thought. It's been vacant for years and rumor has it that it will be auctioned in the spring." Mrs. Hill showed Marci a bunch of pale and creamy helichrysums. "Here, look at these. I think we can make something pretty."

"These flowers are named after the Greek sun god, Helios. The name means sun gold," Marci explained to no one in particular, picking up the bunch of flowers and examining each petal. "Greg, did you know in the Victorian era, a bride getting married in the winter would always carry a Tussy Mussie? She would grow the flowers herself in the summer and dry them in the attic to make her wedding bouquet. There was no such thing as a local floral shop." Marci walked over to the wall and picked up a dried cluster of baby's breath, holding it for effect next to the helichrysums. "I think I'll just buy the dried flowers and make the bouquet myself," Marci decided on the spot. "I don't know why I didn't think of this before."

"Sure, honey, you could do that, and it would be real sweet," Mrs. Hill cooed to Marci. To Greg she added, shaking her head, "Just couldn't get her away from that farm. She sure learned a lot that summer." Mrs. Hill walked out of the storage room with a smirk on her face.

A veil of melancholy momentarily shadowed Marci's face, but then a broad smile lit her small, regular features as she ignored Mrs. Hill's sarcasm. "Yes, I did, Mrs. Hill. I learned how to trust again. Angela was a remarkable woman." Abruptly, she turned to Greg. "Let's take a walk by the farm while it's still light out." Marci was already pulling on her mittens. "We'll come back tomorrow to finish picking out the flowers. Come on, Greg, let's go."

Puzzled, he hesitated. "Sure, sweetie, but what's the rush? I've never seen you so excited. You must have really loved that place. I'm surprised you never mentioned it before." Greg was finishing his sentence as she swept him to the car, leaving Mrs. Hill standing in her shop, a quizzical expression on her plump face.

Marci sat in silence, trying to find the right words to tell Greg about Angela. She remembered her vibrant, long, red, curly hair and her throaty laughter. She remembered how she envied her lifestyle. All winter long she would work at her potter's wheel creating beauty from lumps of clay, forming and reforming the mass until it was uniquely hers. She would give up her soul to each piece of her work. She taught Marci how to center the clay on the wheel and how to master her own life, how to love again. Angela had told Marci that she reminded her of the clay on the wheel, that summer, soft and malleable, ready to take her own unique shape centered around a little piece of Angela's soul.

That summer was spent growing the flowers she would hang to dry, picking each blossom at the height of its beauty. As Marci remembered the attic of the old farm house, the rafters all adorned with upside down hanging bouquets of drying flowers, the sight and smell of Angela seemed to fill the car. She recalled Angela's warm terry cloth robe filled with the scent of dried lavender. Angela had wrapped her in it after they had gotten caught in a surprising summer storm. She could still feel Angela's soft white porcelain skin next to hers, the feeling of her lover. The memories ignited a hidden place in her heart sparking desire. She looked at Greg, wondering, and hoping he would understand.

"Here, Greg, pull up right here." Marci was out the door almost before the car had come to a complete stop. The old house stood covered in snow. The roof above the porch seemed to sag under the weight of the cold silence. The entire farm seemed to be a sleeping extension of the house. Part of the picket fence had been bent low by the snow, and Marci tugged Greg's hand, pulling him into the sweeping white meadow after her. "This is where all the special grasses grew. The cat's tail, the canary grass and the wheat. You had to cut the grasses before they were too ripe or you would lose all the blossoms."

Greg trudged in the snow behind Marci, happy to see her so excited and elated. They approached a towering group of pine trees at the edge of the meadow. "Isn't it magic in here?" Marci's face glowed from the cold and exercise. "Once we tried to hide here from a sudden summer storm, but finally made a run for the house. We were drenched. I still love the smell of pine and lavender."

Greg looked around the natural pine enclosure with its fairy tale quality. The pine scent and the dark encompassing closeness of the tall trees made it seem like the inside of a mysterious castle. The trees were so close and thick that the snow barely touched the forest floor in here. He breathed deeply, the smell of the pines cleansing. He imagined the summer here and the lavender, Marci mentioned, growing nearby. She picked up a handful of fallen pine needles. "Each year a new layer falls, covering the earth with

## Seeking Solitude

Why didn't he just shut up? Terry was in no mood to be stuck on the chair lift with this chatty stranger. The five minutes they had already been suspended in the air were beginning to seem like an eternity. This man was continuing to tell her his life story. Terry wanted to pull his red turtleneck sweater up over his mouth to stop his constant genial chatter.

"You know," he continued, "I never thought I'd finally have the courage to separate from my wife. These days up here, alone, have really given me some time to think. Are you married?"

"No," Terry mumbled, staring down at her skis and wishing it were colder so she would have an extra layer of ski clothing to pull up over her face and hide.

A strange sad loneliness suddenly filled the pit of her stomach. Both of her children had grown up skiing on this mountain and right now she missed them terribly. This feeling puzzled as well as amused her since at this very moment they were both skiing somewhere on these slopes. Her daughter, with her brand new husband, and her son, with his girlfriend, were all here for the special occasion. She watched the little tots ski down the slopes bundled in the latest neon hot pinks and canary yellows, all under the protective snowplow positions of their mothers and fathers. Those years with her own children had flown faster than a downhill slalom course. Terry suddenly realized that the fellow next to her was still talking.

"I'm really not sure what I want out of life now that my kids are grown. I really love my wife. I thought we'd grow old together but now, out of the clear blue sky, she wants to be a landscape painter. She's gone back to school and her friends are really weird. There's also Sandy. It started out as just a fling and now, well now, I really think I love them both. Have you ever been married?"

"No," Terry lied, hoping he would finally get the hint that she did not feel like talking.

She was lost in her own thoughts. Swaying her skis back and forth in the breeze, she watched the snow melt off the tips and drip to the ground below.

"After my wife and I dropped the last kid off at school, we went home and she started converting one of the bedrooms into a loft. All she talked about was lighting and shadows and how Roger, her instructor, really loved her work, and well, Sandy, she was just my secretary but she really understood about all the pressures I went through to put those kids through school. It's not easy raising kids today. Think twice before you ever get married and have a family but you're probably not interested in that. A career woman, am I right?"

"Right," said Terry absent-mindedly.

Another wave of desolation and loneliness swept over her as she remembered dropping her youngest son off at college. For a moment, she could have been in that empty hotel room again feeling more alone than she had ever felt in her life. She had paced up and down in that tiny room. Although she was filled with joy and happiness, there was no husband with whom to share that joy. Her life had been in suspension.

Noisily coming to life, the lift machinery broke her meandering thoughts and began to move them forward.

"Gee, looks like we're moving again. Thanks for listening. What would you do if you were in my shoes?" He suddenly sounded very weak and vulnerable.

Terry, until now looking down at the talkative stranger's ski boots, turned in the chair to face him. He was attractive, in a late middle-aged kind of way. His hair was graying. He had kind gentle features with sad blue eyes and a slight scar above his right eye. She wondered what Brian would have looked like had he lived to be fifty. Would he have had the same beautiful smile and white teeth, the perpetually tanned skin? Why did he have to die and leave her widowed? Why?

"Don't know," Terry said instinctively touching his cheek to wipe away a wet drop of melted snow or a tear, she wasn't sure which.

"You're sweet and cute. What did you say your name was?"

"I didn't."

"Well, it was really great talking with you. Have you skied the new peak yet? That's where I'm headed. Maybe we can take a run together. No strings attached. My life is already too complicated."

"No," Terry sighed, lifting up the safety bar and getting ready to burn off this feeling.

"If you like to ski alone, I understand. It's great. I'm really enjoying it too. See you down at the bottom. I'm staying at the Base Lodge."

"Wonderful," Terry said, almost to herself.

She flew down the mountain, enjoying the freedom and exhilaration that made skiing one of her favorite sports. The wind and the speed blew away the nagging feeling that had been pestering her all day. She got back into the lift line hoping that her next partner would be silent and that the lift would take them quickly to the top.

The young man beside her looked amiable and quiet. He reminded her of Brian, many years ago, when he was her high school sweetheart. They were soon being whisked to the top of the mountain as quickly as she had hoped.

"Beautiful day, isn't it?" Terry beamed, still euphoric from the run down the mountain.

"Sure is. This is my last day of winter break and I'm going to make the best of it." He smiled and looked younger still.

"I'm getting married tomorrow afternoon," Terry blurted out.

"Congratulations," the young man wished, never looking up while studying his trail map.

"I'm not sure if I'm doing the right thing," Terry sighed, uncertainly.

"Bummer." The young man looked down and flipped the snow off his skis.

"But I'm really pretty sure, I think. He's younger than me, and he wants a family. I'm forty-five."

"Bummer." The young man squirmed uncomfortably in the seat as he lifted the safety bar, preparing to depart much too soon.

"But it will all work out. It defines the present, you know?" Terry called out after him.

"Sure," he said, skiing off with only the present in mind. "Have a good one."

"I will, I think," Terry said as she lifted her sunglasses up onto the top of her head.

The sun started to fall behind the mountain and dark shadows were weaving their stripes across the white slopes. She knew this last run would be icy even on this unseasonably warm day. She tucked her sunglasses into an inside pocket, promising to pay attention to the icy patches and moguls. As she skied to the cutoff in the woods, a path she was sure would bring her right to her doorstep, she wondered why all the things she loved and desired left her somewhat terrified. With the fading light creating its own ever-changing pathways, it was difficult to find the cutoff at this hour, but she knew this mountain intimately. Why couldn't she feel so certain about the new path her life was about to take?

Skiing triumphantly right up to the door, she savored that feeling of security. Stepping out of her skis, she clomped up the stairs. David had built a roaring fire and was sound asleep on the couch. She watched him for a moment, amazed at his ability to sleep whenever necessary, something he had learned to do in medical school. She kissed him tenderly on the forehead and he opened his eyes.

"Are the kids back in yet, Hon?" she asked anxiously looking around.

"Your babies are out shopping for dinner. They're going to cook tonight."

David watched Terry nervously looking out the window at the quickly darkening landscape.

"It's starting to snow again. Maggie hasn't gotten here yet, has she?"

"No, she hasn't, but don't worry, she'll be here. Remember it's market week and she probably didn't leave the office until three. She'd never miss her big sister's wedding. You look cold. Why don't you sit by the fire?"

That feeling Terry couldn't pinpoint was beginning to creep back into her. She shivered. The house was so quiet; so unlike the joyful camaraderie of the past with a house full of children. Soon it would be just she and David. Maybe, just maybe, another child. The odds for that were not promising. She was, after all, forty-five.

"I love you David," she whispered, bending again to kiss his cheek.

"Do you know tomorrow's the longest night of the year? It's four o'clock and already almost dark. I'm so glad the kids are all here. Did they like skiing the new peak?" Terry had begun to pace back and forth, anxiously looking out the window.

"I'm sure they had a blast. Come, sit down on the couch and get warm." David sat up and made room for Terry.

"I didn't see them once. You should have come out today. The conditions were excellent," Terry said, snuggling into his arms.

"You know I would have loved to, but I had three hard cases to diagnose and tomorrow's going to be a wash." David was warm and content against Terry's chilly body.

"A wash?" Terry sat up straight and looked at David in the dim light.

"You know what I mean. I just won't be able to get any work done. It's a big day." David ruffled the top of her wet hair. The snowflakes sticking to her bangs had begun to melt.

"Well you could always stay home and work. We could cancel our plans," Terry said with an ease she didn't feel.

"Are we getting a little nervous and jittery? I love you and tomorrow we're going to be married. I've thought this thing through many times." David smoothed the wet bangs off her face.

"I know you have David, but are you sure?" Terry made herself comfortable and let David continue to play with her hair.

"Are you?" Not looking at Terry, David was staring off into the fire.

"Yes, but you know me. I'm impulsive. You're the analytical one."

Terry was very aware that David's hand now rested motionless on her forehead.

"I wouldn't call living together for five years rushing into anything," David began.

"But what if I were to leave your practice? You know, just go off and maybe learn to paint landscapes."

"Landscapes? I've never even seen you hold a paintbrush in your hand."

"Well, no, but I've published poetry and short stories. What if I decide to go for my Master's?" Terry looked up at David almost pleadingly.

"Hon, you know you're the most important part of my life and an integral part of my practice. I couldn't hire a better office manager." David was using his best reassuring doctor voice.

"Bummer," was the only reply Terry could think of at the moment.

Just then the door burst open and four young adults with arms full of grocery bags began to dominate the conversation.

"Mom, you're getting married tomorrow. Here, put the chicken away."

Terry was up in an instant and smiling. She was euphoric when all her kids were together. "God, at least take your jackets off," she mother-henned them.

"Isn't this exciting? Where's the big soup pot? We're cooking!"

"David, she's all yours! Mom, come and help me chop the onions. I hate chopping onions; they make me cry."

Terry took control of the onions just as Maggie burst through the door. In tears, she hugged her sister, and best friend, Maggie.

"What in God's name are you crying about, Terry?"

"Oh it's just the onions. Not really! I was worried that you might not be able to make it."

"Miss this wedding? Terry, you know there will be two of us saying 'I Do' tomorrow."

"Two of you? Hey David, there's four of us as well," Terry's daughter piped in. "That makes a total of six. Are you ready for this David?"

David got up and hugged Maggie. Terry watched and wiped her onion tears aside. "Yes, I think I truly am." David grinned as he took a tissue to Terry's eyes. "I truly love you all. Your mom in particular." He took Terry in his arms and kissed her passionately while the rest of his ready-made family hooted, hollered and banged on pots.

"Thanks sweetheart, I truly needed that just now," Terry murmured through her tears.

Terry's mood lightened. The frenzied activity in the kitchen soon became a group project seasoned with a flourish of wine and laughter. Terry cherished the times they were all together. These moments had become a rare event. She tried not to think beyond the present; unfortunately, as soon as the meal was over and everyone appeared content, her thoughts turned to tomorrow. She looked around the room. Heads began to nod, as one by one they dozed by the fire. Only Terry was still filled with nervous energy.

"I can't sleep at all. I'm going for a walk. Maybe the fresh air will put me to sleep." Terry was already at the door and putting on her coat.

"Want some company?" David yawned from the couch.

"No, Hon, I'm just going to walk over to the trail and back. I need to unwind a bit. I won't be long."

Terry walked out into the crisp black air and saw the bright red snow saucers her kids had been fooling around with after dinner as they tried to recapture a little piece of their youth. She picked one up by the handle and carried it with her to the darkened slope.

The night was smooth and soft and black as she set out seeking solitude. The crunch of snow beneath her boots was comforting. It was the only sound breaking the stillness in the woods. The discovery of her absolute aloneness was assuring and astonishing. She walked out to the clearing of the trail and heard the distant sound of the snow cats grooming the mountain. They hummed in the darkness like the ghosts of a distant symphony. Big wet snowflakes had begun to fall again and were soon coming down in thick clumps, turning her vision into a collage of white and black.

Terry brushed the snow off the trail sign with her mitten, Solitude Peak, and now it really was just that. Looking up into the sky, she saw the glowing full moon emerge from behind the confinement of rapidly moving black clouds. It appeared as if someone had just opened the gates to heaven, as the moon illuminated the mountain. She looked up to the top of the trail where she saw the headlights of the snow cat staring strangely down, the only light in the darkness in that direction. The orange glow of its headlights made Terry feel as if some God-like creature were staring down at her with absolute certainty, seeing into her very soul, recording her doubts and her fears, and knowing exactly what she would say and do.

The moon was slowly slipping back into the dark abyss of the cloudy skies when the snow cat began to bear steadfastly down the mountain. Terry suddenly sat in the snow saucer and pushed off. In the spinning darkness, her world became a kaleidoscope of dizzying black and white through which she saw things so clearly. She was her own rainbow! Laughing and spinning all the way down the slope, she felt the power within merge with the power above and vowed to find the right words, someday, to turn the blazing chaos of her life's darkness and light into an open book complete with full moons, random clouds, and David.

# A Seasonal Education

The crisp fall air was strikingly refreshing, especially after a three-hour lecture course in a classroom where the average steam heated temperature was 82 degrees Fahrenheit. The campus workmen were busy blowing the freshly fallen leaves into huge piles at the top of the hill. The thought suddenly occurred to her to jump into one of those piles. It had been years since she'd taken the plunge; so jump she did. A curious thing then happened. The leaves encircled her in one enormous ball and slowly began to roll down the hill. She wasn't frightened, but rather enjoyed the secure comfortable containment of the familiar autumn smells. The ball of leaves moved very slowly, and soon she began to feel a bit chilly. She pulled her pink wool coat tightly round her and watched ice crystals form in her habitat. They encircled her like stars in the comforting darkness. The dormant chill of the new crystal snow gave her time to reflect until she was no longer encircled by the snow, but had become one with the giant snowball rolling ever so slowly down the hill. She was peaceful and serene until she felt a drip. The ice was melting. Her pink coat, having been absorbed by the melting snow, burst into a ball of pink blossoms. She now rolled serenely down the hill, proud of this latest accomplishment and quite sure of her beauty. She was one great big beautiful ball. Soon the wind picked up and her blossoms began to float in the breeze. Although she was temporarily saddened and began to cry, her tears turned her into a lush verdant round topiary with all new green foliage. She enjoyed this part the most. She just kept growing. There seemed to be no end to what she could do, until one day she noticed one of her leaves turning gold. It was the same day she arrived with a thud at the bottom of the campus hill. The dean handed her the long awaited degree, and she ate it. She needed the pulp. Her golden years had begun. The dean just shook his head, unable to identify this strange entity to whom he had just bestowed a degree. He thought, to himself, it might be time to change the fertilizer or at least the degree requirements. Once again, a curious event occurred. As soon as she digested the degree, her foliage began to turn into a brilliant array of vivid autumn colors swaying luxuriously in the breeze. The wind once again picked up and, one by one, her leaves began to fall and scatter into many far away places. Some even landed in a heap at the top of the hill where a scared, lonely, female student stood ready to jump in. She smiled with satisfaction as she looked up to the top of the hill. Good Lord, she could not even recognize herself.

## Wake Me To Sleep

We are all Claire's co-workers. As people always do, when they are put together to earn a living, we exchange our daily good mornings and pleasantries, but all of us secretly admire Claire. She seems to possess a certain strength and dauntless perseverance. There is a smile on her face every morning, even though we know the rumor of her husband's latest affair has just reached her ears, a bit of information casually mentioned by a well-meaning associate. We are not her confidants, just her co-workers. We hear and observe only bits and pieces of Claire's life.

"Yes, sweetheart. Of course, darling. It will be all right, honey." She whispers these softly spoken affirmatives to her children and her husband in hushed tones. Always, she is quiet.

"We all go through difficult periods in life." She speaks these words as much to us as she does to soothe her own painful soul.

The word inspirational was invented to describe this woman. Through all her hardships, and there are many, she continues to maintain her calm, soothing smile and gentle accepting manner.

It is her gentle smile that I see now, while I lie here quietly in the warmth of my own bed, thinking of Claire.

The glimpses we get of Claire's life flash through my mind. We, ourselves, are a new experience for Claire. Claire enters our world of office work, and we love her. She is always there, ready and eager to do whatever is needed. She seems to balance her new career and home life, and do it so well. We know that things are rough at home; her husband has lost his job and there are bills to pay. We know her home is for sale. Without wanting to know, we know too much. We hold her in reverence. She goes home to cook meals for her family of four, and we go to pick up take-out.

That slender, frail, powerhouse of emotional stamina never seems to need anyone. Her big brown sorrowful eyes are all the more poignant because of their lack of adornment. Claire wears no make-up. Her waif-like appearance is made complete by her long, straight, black hair. She appears so young until you look into those eyes, deep into those serious eyes.

Claire never asks for a favor. We, therefore, never ask if there is anything we can do to help. She seems to grow thinner and more vulnerable every day, but she continues to keep smiling.

"No one ever promised us life would be easy." She seems to have a daily litany of inspirational phrases. But we know life should not be that difficult. What amazes us is that coping, for Claire, seems so easy.

In a corporate office, such as ours, gossip travels fast. Everyone is acquainted with the fact that Claire's husband fools around. We are also aware of her teenage son, and drugs, and his two suicide attempts. Her son is having a rough time, but Claire is miraculous. She courageously takes one day at a time.

A dream-like quality always surrounds Claire. There is an aura of serenity about her. She never seems to ruffle, ever, until today.

Claire needs a ride home. It is a cold, raw and wet, bone-chilling day. We all jump at the chance to be of some assistance; it is the first time we can ever recall her asking for a favor. I volunteer.

The beating of the rain against the windshield and the swooshing of the wipers are the only noise in the car for the entire ride. Claire is, as usual, very quiet. As we pull up to her home, Claire screams and bolts out of the car. Illuminated by my headlights, lying on the road, is her gray cat, Misty. Misty has apparently been struck by a car on this awful night. I watch silently as Claire picks up the little injured creature and cuddles him against her breast, trying to warm him and protect him from the cold and rain. I believe he is dead. She begins to walk along the road still cuddling her cat. I get out of the car to follow her, but her walk quickens and she begins to run. She is running, running to somehow quiet the pent up rage building within her. She is biting her lip and trying desperately not to cry. I have never seen her cry. She has to compose herself, gain control, smile. As I run along side her, Claire stops and turns, about to speak to me. The rage building in her heart is about to reach her lips when the headlights of an oncoming car flood our vision. Her face is a mask of terror. Her lips are quivering. Her eyes are glazed and her skin is pale; she is flushed with anger. But the car passes, and it is cold and dark again. Claire begins to walk silently back to her home cuddling and stroking her dead pet.

"It will be all right, darling. It will be all right." She continues to say. She is not speaking to me. She does not even realize I am still there.

I pull my hood up over my head, trying to shut out the wind and the rain, trying to make the night not as cold and dark and empty as it suddenly appears, trying not to look at Claire. She has refused my hug. She is smiling that quiet, gentle smile again. I am no longer inspired. I am only chilled, chilled and frightened to be here watching Claire.

It is funny now, many years later, lying here in the warmth of my own bed that I am thinking of Claire. I have not seen her in over ten years. My own teenage son has just come in the front door rousing me from that state of semi-slumber and dream-like thought by the comforting sound of the closing front door and his soft footsteps climbing the carpeted stairs. I wait for a kiss good night. I can now close my eyes and sleep. Funny how he must always wake me to sleep. Funny, why now, I remember Claire.

## Vegetable Fajitas At Vinney's Bar & Grill

Tricia was in a crummy mood. Her feet hurt and the tips were really awful today. Twenty-seven years old and still waiting on tables in this hole in the wall, she sat down at long last, kicked off her sneakers and rubbed her aching feet. It was a real slow night. The Monday night truckers had long since passed through. Her shift was over in almost an hour; maybe she'd get lucky and no one else would come in today. With a little bit of luck she could be soaking in her tub by midnight. At least she didn't have to work that horrible midnight to six shift. That's when all the weirdoes really came in, half of them drunk or on drugs these days after their forays into the Big Apple. That shift was full of pigs. They didn't tip, they left a mess, and they were always grabbing at her. Yuck, just the thought made her ill. She heard the phone ringing but knew either Vinney or Sophie would pick it up. They were closer. She stared out at the horizon. The tall buildings of New York City still smiled their twinkling city eyes at her but they had stopped beckoning long ago. She had tried to make it as a dancer, Miss Dottie's cute little star, but when reality hit, she couldn't even land a job, unless you count that stint on the cruise ship. Oh, what's the use of daydreaming? The city was as far out of her reach as it had been when she was a little girl. Sometimes she was happy her mom died five years ago, with the hope still in her heart that Tricia would be a star. She felt so guilty every time she had those feelings but what the hell! The truth was now she was alone, an adult orphan waiting on tables for a living while trying to decide what to do with the rest of her life. She felt as if she was drifting into a sort of fog. She barely heard Vinney speaking.

"Hey Pumpkin," he yelled from the kitchen, "can you fill in for Juanita tonight and work straight through until the breakfast crew comes in? Her kids are sick again."

"Oh, no!" Tricia sighed with deep exhaustion. Juanita's kids were always sick. And why does he call me Pumpkin? Just because my hair is red, or orange as he calls it, but at least it's natural, not like Sophie's with her dark roots showing every three weeks. Pumpkin ... it brought back too many memories that weren't even hers. Memories that she'd picked up from her mom. Treasured words from the father she never knew. He had called her Pumpkin the day she was born. Her mom had told her the story so many times she cherished it as her own memory. Then three months later he was dead in the jungles of Vietnam. She wished, deep in her heart, that they were both here right now, both her parents, to help her through this period of her life.

"Oh, God, help me," she sighed. She wanted to cry and scream and shout, but all she yelled back was, "Sure, Vinney, I don't need to sleep like normal people. I can work and work and work and just keep on working. I'm the original Energizer."

"Come on, Pumpkin, it's quiet tonight, it's Monday. Besides..."

"I'll do it! I'll do it! I'll do it Vinney, just stop calling me Pumpkin."

Vinney came out of the kitchen wiping his greasy hands on his apron. He always smelled like fried food. Even when he was showered and dressed, although the only time she had ever seen him dressed was at his wife's funeral. Vera had died two years ago. She still felt sorry for him; that's probably why she kept agreeing to work more, stay longer. What the hell. She would never be a dancer. At twenty-seven she felt she was over the hill. She pulled her green eyes away from the city and looked at Vinney, a real meat and potatoes kind of guy.

"What's wrong with Pumpkin? Vera always used to call you Pumpkin and I thought you loved it." Vinney looked as if he was about to cry. He wished Vera were here to help him out. God did he miss her.

"Oh, I'm just tired today, Vinney. I was watching my sister's kids all weekend and I guess I was just looking forward to some rest, that's all."

"You need a couple of your own, Pumpkin." Vinney blushed as soon as he'd said the words and regretted them immediately. He had not meant to antagonize her or get personal.

"Right, Vinney, just what I need now. I can't even support myself with this crummy job." As soon as she said it, she felt like a heel. Vinney worked like a slave making this bar & grill work. It was his baby. He and Vera never had kids of their own. Vera's cancer claimed that chance as well. Why had she snapped at him? He was just trying to be nice. What was the purpose of it all? Working away at life and having cancer beat you up like a bunch of thugs. For some reason, her old Baltimore catechism flashed through her mind. Then all the big questions had answers. Today no questions had any answers, only more questions. It was so simple then.

Just then the door jingled and a young, well-dressed man walked over to the counter. Sophie went to take his order while Tricia put her shoes back on and Vinney shook his head in disbelief. My God! The girl had bunions at her age. What did they make those dancers do? Standing on your toes was just not meant to be. It was not natural ... but it was beautiful, Vinney had to concede that. Oh, what did he know anyway?

"I see you have chicken fajitas on the menu. Do you think you could whip me up a vegetable fajita? I'm a vegetarian and it's late and I don't really have the time to look for another restaurant. This stop is so convenient right outside the Lincoln Tunnel. Seems I literally flew through the tunnel this time but came out starving. That's not usually how it is."

Tricia saw him smile and it was breathtaking. She quickly tidied up her apron and smoothed her hair and went over to help Sophie.

"Vinney, I think we can do that, don't you?"

Vinney was already in the back slicing every vegetable he could find that wasn't a potato.

Soon their late night guest was mopping his last tortilla in the grease and thanking them profusely. He got up to leave and as if remembering something long forgotten, turned around, and left Tricia a huge tip.

"See you around Tricia," he smiled as he walked out of the door.

"Friend of yours, Pumpkin?" Vinney asked quietly.

"Never saw him before in my life." Tricia's eyes followed him out the door. She stood there stunned and numbly stuffed the bill into her apron.

"Well, then, how did he know your name?"

"It's right here on my name tag, genius. Oh Sophie, I'm in love. I could really love a man who orders vegetable fajitas."

"Why?" Vinney asked, incredulous at the change in Tricia's behavior.

"Oh, because he'd be kind and gentle and treat me like a lady. He must be sensitive and bright and well educated. Look at the way he was dressed."

"You can never tell, Pumpkin; some of those yuppie types dress real nice just to go downtown and score a drug deal."

"Oh Vinney, he was carrying a briefcase. He was a professional, I'm sure."

"Oh sure, a professional what? He's probably married," Sophie remarked only half jokingly. "You're lucky we had all those leftover vegetables from the stew special, Vinney. I'm calling it a night. You and Pumpkin can take care of the late crew tonight. I'm going to drop this cake off at Juanita's."

Vinney always sent left over food home with his employees. Juanita in particular really needed all the help she could get. Tricia was still whirling around when two women walked in and sat down at one of the tables. "Not the ordinary late night crowd tonight," she thought. She went over to take their order.

"We hear you make wonderful vegetable fajitas here," said the older, motherly looking woman whose gray hair was pulled neatly into a bun.

Tricia felt her mouth drop open as she heard Sophie's footsteps going out the door.

"Who told you that?" Tricia managed to ask as she regained her composure.

"Oh, Raffy did. He said in case we got through the tunnel real fast this time, there was a great place to stop for vegetable fajitas right at the exit."

Tricia walked slowly back to the kitchen a little apprehensively.

"Vinney ... do we have anymore of those vegetables left. I've got an order for two more vegetable fajitas." Tricia was playing with one of her escaped tendrils, contemplating the evening's events.

"No problem, Pumpkin. I'll whip them up in no time."

Tricia set their table and eyed them curiously. The women both smiled at Tricia and seemed absolutely radiant. Tricia began to relax. The younger woman put her briefcase up on the table. God, it looked just like the one that man, Raffy, she thought they called him, had left with just minutes ago. They must all work together or something. Weird stuff!

Vinney brought out the steaming plates of vegetable fajitas and the younger woman looked at him benevolently. Tricia was sure they knew each other. Then the women began to eat with laughter and gusto.

"Goodbye Tricia," said the women as they left the bar & grill. "That was wonderful."

Vinney looked at the disappearing ladies and smiled. "Looks like we may have to put vegetable fajitas on the menu, Pumpkin. Friends of yours again?"

"No, not really ... yet they seemed to know my name just like Raffy did, and I was so comfortable around them. They didn't even seem like strangers. Actually, the younger one looked like she knew you."

"Never saw her before in my life. But I thought you didn't know the last guy?"

"I didn't."

"Then how do you know his name?"

"They told me."

"Oh, trying to get a fix-up going? Don't go messing with any strangers. I used to be a state trooper. There can be a lot of well-dressed kooks out there, you know."

"I didn't know you were ever a state trooper, Vinney."

"Well, I don't really talk about it much. Did two years of law school after college."

"You went to college?"

"Sure did! Why are you so surprised? Do I look like some kind of Bozo? Just because I don't wear a suit all day doesn't mean I don't have a brain. Vera and I met in college." Vinney stopped and wiped his eyes on his apron. "Onions, you know ... they always make your eyes tear." Vinney paused awkwardly, embarrassed by his tears. "It's still hard, you know ... sometimes. We took a gamble on this place. Vera was a swell cook. I bet she would have loved vegetable fajitas."

"Oh, I'm sorry, Vinney. I never, I never... Oh, I'm so sorry."

Just then, an old man came in the door. He sat down at the first table, looking rather glazed.

"That tunnel is getting to be just too much for me, Tricia," he said with a wink of his eye. "Even on these special occasions." The old man used her name as comfortably as if he had known her all her life.

Tricia made a mental note to take her nametag off, but then forgot about it as soon as the older gentleman smiled. He had the same radiant smile as Raffy and the older women.

"Are you related to Raffy?"

"Well, sort of ... let's just say he works for me. He told me about your vegetable fajitas. So did my wife, Lilith; she was in here before with a friend."

"Let me go and see if we have anymore left." Tricia almost stumbled as she tried to back away from the kind older gentleman without taking her eyes off him.

"Hey Vinney, this is too weird. There's an old man who wants vegetable fajitas now. Says he's a friend of all the rest of them. I'm getting spooked."

Vinney started rummaging though the shelves. "Here we go, Pumpkin, two more veggie fajitas coming up."

"Two? Did I say he wanted two?"

Tricia started to make her way back to the table, but before she even reached her destination the old man smiled and said, "That's right, two."

"God, he may be old, but he had the hearing of a bionic man," Tricia thought.

As the gentleman was finishing, he called Tricia over. She handed him the bill, assuming that's what he wanted, and started to walk away. The old man's hand reached out to grab hers and she felt a shiver run up and down her spine. Oh, no! Not another dirty old man! But his hand felt warm and tender, not cold and dirty. He merely pressed a note into her palm.

"Raffy said to give you this, Tricia." He winked at her knowingly. "And by the way, sometimes my competition likes to follow me around. They're dishonest, to say the least. Not as nice as I am, but they've been around just as long. Take care of yourself. You can handle them." With that weirdo comment he winked again and walked out the door.

Too frightened even to open the note, she ran into the kitchen and stuffed it into her apron pocket.

"Vinney ... what are you doing?"

"Eating a vegetable fajita Pumpkin. Want some? They're not bad..."

The door jingled and Tricia ran out. "Oh, now here it comes," she thought. A group of rowdy teenagers was settling into a booth. Why did she agree to this second shift?

"Raffy sent us," said the oldest. "Said you could really love a man who ate vegetable fajitas."

Tricia turned the color of her hair. That bastard! Was this some kind of a joke?

"Come here, Pumpkin!"

Tricia's blood turned to ice water.

First they all knew her name, then they ... oh, God, what would be next?

"Aren't we the cute little ballerina? Dance for us, Pumpkin! Dance for us Tricia!" said the mangiest of the crew.

"Make us some vegetable fajitas real soon. We're real hungry," hissed one of his cohorts.

Tricia was terrified. These kids were horrible.

"Vinney, Vinney!" Tricia screamed out at the top of her lungs. Vinney came out of the kitchen and looked at Tricia. Her head was lying on the tabletop and she looked as if she were sleeping.

He shook her shoulders gently, "Pumpkin ... Pumpkin, what's up?"

"Oh, Vinney, what's going on? Everyone knows my name, and my nickname and my dreams and ... what are you eating?"

"A vegetable fajita. I thought I'd put them on the menu. Everyone today is so health-conscious. I'm just about a vegetarian anyway, watching my cholesterol and all. And besides, I always wanted to expand the menu a little. Here, take a bite. No one's here and your shift is almost over. Want me to drive you home? Juanita should be here any minute."

Tricia stood up and shook her head in disbelief.

"Juanita's kids are sick, aren't they?"

"What? That's news to me."

"Didn't she call about an hour ago before all these weird customers started arriving and you asked me to take her shift?"

"Pumpkin, we've had no customers for the last hour. I've been cooking, Sophie's been cleaning up, and you took a nap. You looked so tired, I just let you sleep. Here, put your shoes on."

Tricia looked at her shoes and started to cry.

"What's wrong, Pumpkin?"

"I think I'm losing it, Vinney. I had the weirdest dream. I'm even working in my dreams. Vinney, did you ever go to college?"

Vinney blushed.

"Were you ever a state trooper?"

Vinney blushed some more.

"Well, tell me the truth ... or ... or ... I quit."

"Pumpkin, yes, yes ... sort of surprises you, doesn't it?"

"No ... it was in my dream."

"My personnel file was in your dream?"

"Oh, Vinney, I better get going home. I think I'm over-exhausted."

"Want a drive home?"

"No thanks... Oh, what the hell. Sure." The minute she said the word "hell" she felt a shiver run up and down her spine. She had been cursing too much recently and meant to stop.

"Tell me about being a state trooper and ... what ever made you decide to open up this bar & grill?"

"Money. Vera and I thought it would make a lot of money and it does, but that's not enough."

Tricia tossed her apron over the hook and reached for her coat. She remembered her tips and ran back to fish them out of her apron pocket. She looked in shock at the one hundred dollar bill in her hand. A little bit of paper, folded in half, also was in her hand. Shaking and weak in the knees, she forced herself to open it.

"You could love a man who ate vegetable fajitas," was all it said.

Tricia turned and Vinney was smiling. He was always doing wonderful things for all his employees, but this was too much of a coincidence. He couldn't have caused her dream ... could he?

"Did you put this in my apron, Vinney?"

"What?"

"This note and this hundred dollar bill."

"What note and what hundred dollar bill?" He was laughing and his smile was contagious, almost radiant.

"I think we should talk about your future tonight, not my past. What do you want to do with your life?"

Tricia started to smile even though she was on the verge of tears. No one had ever asked her that question. She walked out with her coat over her arm. Vinney put his arm around her shoulders to ward off the chilly evening air.

Somewhere in the not too distant past and already into the future, Raffy and company smiled angelically as they whirled back through the tunnel.

## Scarlet Begonias

Blood brothers since third grade, Drew and Tony had grown to be an inseparable pair of teenagers. Both sported shocking red hair and freckles, making them look more like brothers than best friends. Memories of that day of brotherhood, many autumns ago, stood out vividly in Drew's mind. Now, his fist clenched the tiny scout knife they had used to make those brave incisions, that razor sharp declaration of their friendship. He could almost feel Tony's presence, here in the park, on the edge of the bridge where they had played as kids. This had been their favorite hideout, an enclosed glen, under a canopy of trees, where the sun played games, streaming through the branches, creating bold patterns of alternating light and darkness below the bridge. Here they would toss rocks, float paper boats or strum their guitars as they got older. Something about the stream's continuity, yet ever-changing demeanor, intrigued the boys. It seemed to calm them when their moods were turbulent and inspire them when summer doldrums weighted their spirits with lethargy. In the silence, Drew could hear Tony strumming his guitar and singing his favorite Grateful Dead tune, "Scarlet Begonias." Only thirteen then, they had memorized all the words. Spreading his fingers through his hair in anguish, Drew wanted to turn the clock back to simpler days, days of hanging out and singing in the park, on the bridge.

He needed this time to think and be alone. Sitting down on a stone bench, he tried to focus his attention by looking for a special object highlighted by the sun. This was a game they had played as altar boys in the sixth grade, recapturing with awe and wonder God's decision to momentarily illuminate a piece of nature like a priceless jewel. Only, today, he was alone. He, Drew Smith, the senior voted most likely to succeed, singled out for a bright future, sat alone now without his best friend.

He turned his tear stained eyes to a rock along the path. It stood there, staunchly solid, aglow in a silvery splash of sunlight penetrating the protective covering of trees. He moaned deeply, knowing he needed some of that stability right now. He listened instinctively for the sound of Tony's infectious, encouraging laughter; the laughter that always chased away their worries with fantastic dreams of tomorrow. It was gone. He shook his head to stop the pain. Clenching and unclenching his fists, he squeezed his eyes shut and then forced them open, his senses fluctuating precariously between the light and the darkness. The tiny red penknife he had been clenching fell from his hands, unnoticed, to lie blazing on the ground.

A lone maple leaf, well on its way of chameleon-like change to bright crimson, glistened under a delicate spider web that had collected the morning dew. Drew reached out and twirled the fine web around his finger, wondering where the spider had gone and how it would start the monumental task of rebuilding its web. If it were only that easy. An icy fear swept through his body as he stared at the last rays of sun highlighting a pile of dry yellow leaves near his feet. He wanted those rays of warmth to enter his shivering heart. He glanced from the dusty pile of leaves back to the precarious ruby leaf, no longer supported by the friendly web, and wept.

He had not cried at the funeral, surrounded by supportive friends, all wearing red ties, trying, somehow, to stay united in grief. Wrinkled jackets and slacks, pulled out of the backs of closets, had taken the place of cut-off shorts and T-shirts, their painting uniforms for the summer. Young entrepreneurs, their summer painting job had become a huge success, a cause for celebration.

Rubbing his painfully swollen eyes, Drew knew it was time to leave the park. The last slanted ray of sun had singled a large old tree trunk, split and lifeless, but now playing host to new green life in its hollow cavity. A multitude of tiny wild flowers surrounded the craggy stump as it stood there, proud as an ancient cathedral with adoring choirboys at its feet.

Drew bolted to his feet. He knew what he had to do. Trying desperately to hum a few bars of Tony's favorite Dead tune, he headed out of the park, intent on recapturing a spark of the minor comfort he had just experienced here on the edge of the bridge. But the fickle sun had already switched allegiance, and dark shadows began to penetrate the path. A vermilion sunset was screaming as Drew's steps quickened. The tie he had worn all day began to feel like a noose around his neck and he ripped it off, abandoning it in his haste to outrun the shadows. His feet fell like lead, his body not moving fast enough to shed his grief. He tore off his shoes and socks and kept running. The dark shadows began to spill across his white shirt, and he screamed and yelled out Tony's name.

"Don't die, Tony! Please don't be dead," he kept screaming as he raced down the wide avenue and out of the park.

He looked down at his sweat-soaked shirt and remembered the bright red stain that grew there, only days ago, lifeblood leaving his best friend. In a frenzy, he began to rip the shirt off his body, when he saw the flower shop. His face was flushed with pent-up self-hate and sorrow bursting in his veins.

"Scarlet begonias!" He screamed to the frightened clerk behind the counter. "I've got to find them," he continued to shriek as he grabbed the spectacled man by the shirt collar.

"Please," he cried painfully, releasing the man from his grip. Tears ran in torrents down his young cheeks, creating rivulets of sorrow, washing away scabby nicks from this morning's close shave and the coagulated blood of cuts, not yet healed, from the shattered windshield.

"Here, take these," the little man trembled. "They're not begonias, but they're red." He shoved red carnations into Drew's hand, not daring to ask for payment. The flowers blurred Drew's vision. They would have to do. He ran out of the store and into the street as the clerk dialed 911.

"Yes, sir," the clerk replied into the receiver. "He was half undressed and running down the street in the direction of the church."

Drew's blood pumped furiously through his heart. No longer trying to stop the building panic, he dodged and leapt his way through the rush hour traffic. A car screeched to a halt as it grazed his hip, and a loud crash echoed the impact of another car in the rear. Drew heard the sound and felt the pain. He saw the blood begin to drip down his pant leg. Still clutching the red carnations, he began staring at them intently, and then he ripped the last remaining clothes from his body.

"I couldn't even find you Scarlet Begonias," he kept screaming, as he sprinted up the stairs of the cathedral. In his mind, the flashing lights of approaching police cars became one with those at the scene of the accident three days ago. He pushed open the heavy door and ran up the aisle, still clutching the flowers. Startled worshippers and tourists looked in shock at the naked young man racing up the aisle. He must be on drugs or something, they muttered. Some got up and ran out. Some continued to pray. Some stood and stretched their necks to get a better view, but no one tried to stop him. It all happened so fast, they said.

The gentle graying usher stepped out from behind the iron prayer book stand and tried to talk calmly to the crazed, nude, young man running up to the statue of St. Anthony, but by now, Drew's reality was slipping fast.

"I had too much to drink!" He screamed, pulling the prayer stand from the floor. "I killed my best friend!" He shrieked, whirling it over his head and striking the usher. "I should have never gotten behind the wheel," he cried to the lifeless statue of St. Anthony staring down at him.

He never heard the officer yell freeze. The bullet that entered his back, from the police revolver, went through his chest. He glanced down in shock, his hand touching the warm blood draining his life away. Witnesses said a smile crossed his lips as he fell atop the red carnations.

Back in the park, the infinite sun had set. Night deepened the shadows into one dark blanket. The crimson leaf fluttered to the ground, no longer able to hang on without the delicate support of the spider web. It landed in the prime of its beauty on top of the abandoned red pen-knife, both nestled quietly in the park on the edge of the bridge.

# Silent Night

Not much was new in the Kristiani household this Yule. The house was decorated and festive and they would put the tree up tonight as soon as everyone arrived home. Mary, exhausted after a long day at the office, stepped out onto the deck for a breath of the chilly night air. A starless gray lavender blanket covered the heavens, serenely tucking in the moon and the stars for this evening. A pale pink aura escaped the horizon like an insuppressible dream. Mary sighed, lit a cigarette and thought about taking painting lessons in the spring. Joe and the kids would probably think she was being silly. The phone rang inside and shattered her thoughts. It was Joe calling to say he'd be home a little later than expected. Mary knew in her heart he was having an affair, but what good would a confrontation do.

Just last night, Joe had stood out on this same deck for what seemed like a very long time. Life for him seemed just perfect. His job paid him more money than he ever dreamed he would make. He loved his wife and adored his latest girlfriend, even though lately she had been hinting at the possibility of his leaving Mary. It might be time to break it off. But it could wait. Right now the solitary star in the night sky seemed ablaze in his glory. The air was still and black and motionless as if it dared not breathe and disturb the precarious balance.

Their son, Justin, was now on his way home furious with the burdensome weight of adolescence. He walked home beneath the same sky under which his mother dreamt. He looked up into the barren sky where the moon and stars had been given the night off. The sky just glared back oppressively. Sullen, silent and eerie, the heavens appeared encased in a shroud. He tried not to think about his girlfriend's abortion. The alcohol was helping.

His sister, Felicia, had just arrived home, anxious and eager to decorate the tree. Last night had been wonderful. Her first formal dance left her with a lingering radiant glow. She and her date had stood with their arms around each other, and the heavens smiled down on them. One star, no moon, and a warm rosy sheen embraced the landscape. The friendly, blinking star radiated in the black sky, as distant members of the solar system decided not to compete. She was content in her innocence.

The family, finally all together, strung the tangled lights upon the tree and placed each memory filled ornament on with loving care. Memories filled the silent room as Joe lifted his grown daughter to place the angel atop the tree. They wished each other Merry Christmas, exchanged gifts of love, and went their separate ways, each encompassed like an individual glass ornament surrounded with their own memories.

Mary went upstairs to put away her gifts. She sprayed on her favorite perfume, a gift from Felicia and opened the box of potpourri that Justin had made himself. The scent of fragrant spices filled the room. She held the gold and diamond earrings up to her ears and watched them glitter in the mirror. She wondered if Joe had picked them out himself.

Outside in the chilled night air, the black sky still imprisoned the moon and the stars.

## The Family Jewel

Filly watched the blizzard pile huge drifts of snow on the back deck. The view through the sliding glass doors was being quickly obliterated by the fierce diamond-edged white flakes hurling themselves against the glass with unabated fury. The white-out was unrelenting. Cold bitter winds cried through every crevice in the house, determined to help the storm pour out its rage.

She sat snuggled under her light blue afghan, content to keep the fire going nice and steady. Everyone was safe and sound. The boys were out of state with their father visiting Nana. They would not be happy to hear they had missed the snowstorm of the century. Her daughter, Lily, had come home early from the barn, having safely tucked Necromancer, her prized black stallion, under some extra blankets. He would spend the night safe and warm in his stall and in the morning would be eager to romp in the fresh white stuff covering the earth. As Filly played with the tiny tear-shaped iridescent crystal hanging around her neck on a thin gold chain, she felt serenely nostalgic. The evening reminded her so much of her own childhood in the country.

"Come here, sweetie," she called out to Lily. "Let me help you get those riding boots off. I'm so glad you're home."

Filly got up and tugged on Lily's long black boots till they slid off her slender calves. Lily was watching the top of her mother's head as Filly bent over her daughter's boots. Filly fell back in playful exhaustion.

"Mom, you've gotten more white hair. Here let me pull this one out. It's sticking straight up, and besides, Clarissa's mother lets her pull out all her gray hairs."

"Then, I'm surprised she's not bald already." Lily laughed and pushed her mother down onto the soft couch, plopping down next to her. Lily snuggled into her mother's arms, too much on her way to becoming a woman to fit into her lap, but still needing the warmth and softness of her touch.

Filly lovingly caressed and stroked her daughter's long brown curls. Her own hair was turning white just as Lily's would one day; the years really seemed to fly. This seemed like a good time to tell her the story of her great, great-grandmother, Anna Patchenka.

"Do you know how those white hairs are placed Lily, and why and by whom?" Lily turned her head to face her mom, eager to hear another one of her mother's stories.

"They are settled there, one by one, by a very special spirit, and she is very close to you. She was my great grandmother, Anna Patchenka, and she had the most beautiful blue eyes, just like yours." Filly paused now, trying to pick her words very carefully. She did not want to tell Lily too much too soon. She remembered distinctly the awe she felt when she first saw the spirit of Anna Patchenka take shape. Even though the spirit world was rapidly gaining credibility and Lily had studied about it in school, this was a particularly strong spirit, and it guided every woman in their family. Spirituality was still not an easy thing to discuss between parent and child, but with the warmth and security of the fire shielding them from the storm, the moment seemed right. Besides, it was really past the time she should have spoken to Lily; and tonight was perfect.

"You see, my little one, life is really a balance, a fine white thread, a stability, that we must walk with open eyes, an open heart and always an open mind." She paused now to take a deep breath, much as her own mother had paused years ago when telling her the truth. She continued now with Lily's complete attention.

"We must always try to master the art of balancing all three, but it is only by imbalance that we acquire wisdom and the ability to cope with the unforeseen." Filly looked down at her daughter. She could tell by the quizzical expression on her face, that she still did not see the connection between this story and her mom's white hair. She took another deep breath and continued.

"Whenever life becomes too easy, or we become too complacent, the spirit of Anna Patchenka swoops down and pulls out the fine white thread of balance and places it gently into our crown of brown curls as we peacefully sleep. We wake up wiser and more serene, able to walk another fine white line that has already been laid down for us." Lily looked up at her mom; the look of mystery that had shrouded her face moments before had lifted. Filly was going to continue, but Lily's face was aglow with understanding.

"I think I've already seen the spirit, Mom. She comes to me sometimes when I'm riding Necromancer or have just finished a great paper for school. She always tells me I can do anything I set my mind on, no matter what my age. Oh Mom, she's a beautiful spirit. Her long white hair blows in billows on the wind and she rides a fierce white stallion, always bareback. And oh, her face! It is so gentle and radiant and gorgeous, with deep blue eyes like pools of wisdom."

So her daughter had already seen the spirit of Anna Patchenka. Filly decided to finish her daughter's description. "And her body is as young and slender as yours and white as alabaster, and always proudly unclothed."

"Oh Mother, that's right! I have seen her. I have!" Lily was now up and waving her arms and dancing in jubilation. Filly beamed with pride. She was glad she had chosen this moment to tell her daughter, even if she had already seen the spirit. Anna Patchenka was obviously up to her old tricks, already laying out the fine white lines Lily would have to walk.

"Now come here a moment, little one. She is a strong and willful spirit and not easy to pacify. She will continue to test you by always removing the fine white thread just when you've thought you'd achieved perfect balance." Filly wrapped her arms around her daughter and they both snuggled under the well-worn blue afghan.

It really was time to throw another log on the fire. The room had begun to get chilly. The storm outside had subsided. The heavy black evening sky, sliding down to soothe the gentle white blanket on the earth, had turned into a warm gray with the light of the moon and the reflection of the snow. Occasional flurries floated daintily down from the heavens. The evening bore no resemblance to the earlier fury. The world was at peace.

Filly decided she had told her daughter enough about the spirit for now. As she gazed at the passionately blazing fire, she realized that one day soon she would have to tell her daughter the rest of the story. Lily would have to warn the men she loved, warn them to be true and faithful, for that lithe spirit, full of wonder and encouragement, was also an avenger. In their dreams, men chased her young form as she fled through the clouds on her white stallion. Most of them never really wanted to catch her; she was only a dream, but if they turn their fantasies into reality and cheat on the woman they love, the spirit of Anna Patchenka turns to face them. The face of a wizened old toothless hag, turns to stare at them from that wholesome young body and the steel blue eyes penetrate their very soul with guilt. With the sound of her one piercing scream, "Holeda," still ringing in their ears, they never wake up.

Hugging her daughter tighter and clutching her necklace, Filly decided this part of the story could wait. Lily would not see that side of the spirit until she had shed her one, first, perfect, crystal tear of sorrow, crying over a man. Filly would then pass on the necklace to Lily so she too, like all the Patchenka women before her, would wear her tears like diamonds.

"Close your pretty blue eyes, my little one, and just let me hold you. Right now you remind me so much of my great-grandmother."

# Mama Says

The decision had been made; well at least Frankie had made up his mind. He and Monica would spend the night at his cousin Rosalie's house. By tomorrow this blizzard would have cleared and they could continue the long drive home. The skiing conditions had been excellent, but driving all the way back home in this weather did not excite him. Besides, he had other motives. He knew his grandmother was at Rosalie's for a few days. He could already smell the spaghetti sauce simmering. His heart, right now, belonged to a crispy loaf of Italian bread.

Monica had other thoughts as they approached the house. She had met the old lady once, and honestly, she gave her the creeps. She was always staring at her and scrutinizing her every move; but Frankie adored her, so she couldn't be that bad.

They pulled up to the big old colonial house, and sure enough, the smell of garlic, onions and tomatoes filled the air. Mama knew her Frankie was coming. One whiff and he was on cloud nine, filling his senses with the aroma of Mama's Sunday sauce. One whiff and Monica wriggled her nose in distaste. She knew from past experience the scene that would follow. Mama would hug and squeeze Frankie and pinch his cheeks as if he were a baby, and then turn to look at her. Monica always offered her hand politely. The thought of that toothless old hag hugging and kissing her was more than she could cope with. She even expected Monica to call her Mama, now that she and Frankie were engaged.

"Come anda give Mama a biga kiss, anda no calla me grandma, I'ma Mama."

Monica sighed. How bad could anyone be who resembled an ancient Pillsbury doughboy? She would honestly try this time to get to know her better. After all, they were stuck here for the whole weekend. She bent down to the little old lady and offered her cheek. Mama grabbed her around the neck and smothered her with kisses. Frankie, now assured that they were well on their way to friendship, headed out to the kitchen and the waiting loaf of Italian bread.

"I really can't believe him. Seven weeks on the Fit for Life Diet and now he's going to stuff his face with sausage, bread and tomato sauce." Monica groaned her disbelief out loud.

Mama's ears were quick to pick up on the word diet. No one in her family dieted, especially when she cooked.

"Whata you mean diet? Frankie no needa diet. Hesa so skinny now. Hesa gotta eat anda be strong, lika man. Hesa my grandson." Mama was puffed up and proud.

Monica wondered why it was impossible for her to ever say the right thing to Mama. Frankie was still five pounds overweight, but she knew enough to keep her mouth shut on that point. Mama would never understand. Laughingly, she told Mama that everyone who was anyone was on the Fit for Life Diet. It was in now. She was wrong again.

"Whata ya mean? I'ma someone and I'ma on no diet. I'ma fit for 95 years ofa life. Look ata you. You soa skinny. No meat ona you bones," Mama said as she squeezed the flesh on Monica's arm.

Monica quickly, but politely, removed her arm from Mama's clutches. She was beginning to feel that same old sinking feeling. It was useless to try and get to know her. This lady was a creep. She also began to sneeze violently. The cats and dogs that roamed freely through Rosalie's house had begun to set her allergies on fire. Mama eyed her sneezes and runny nose.

"See, you don'ta eat right and now you catcha cold anda you gonna make my Frankie sicka too and that'sa no nice. See, so you gotta eat. Go anna have a meatball ana little shpagetti." Mama was once again all smiles.

Monica grimaced. "I don't eat red meat. It's no good for you and I only eat pasta when we are jogging. Achoo! Achoo! And please, I don't have a cold. It's my allergies. Achoo! How are Frankie and I ever going to sleep in here tonight with those damn cats? Can't you put them outside? I haven't had an allergy shot in over a week!" With this outburst, Monica decided it was time to stop this ridiculous conversation and headed for the spare room to unpack her many bags. Mama waddled behind her in close proximity. So did the three cats. Mama watched her silently as she unpacked her things as well as Frankie's. Her eyes narrowed a little and she began to shake her finger.

"No, no, ashpet, ashpet, you no gonna sleepa with my Frankie! You gotta no wedding band ona you finger, justa that biga rock my Frankie worka so hard to buy fora you. I'ma olda lady anda I no believe you sleepa together till after you weara whita dress in church." Mama stood there with her arms crossed very satisfied.

Monica began to unpack furiously, throwing things down on the bed while constantly shooing off the ever-present curious cats and sneezing. She and Frankie had been living together for over a year, and she was not about to sleep apart just to pacify this old lady.

"I hate these cats. Ever since I had my nose done, my allergies Achoo have been terrible. Achoo!" The moment the words left her mouth, Monica realized she had made a grave slip of the tongue. The old woman's squinty eyes were rudely looking straight at her nose. Why did she have to stare like that? Monica continued to unpack with a vengeance, avoiding the scrutiny, and hoping the slip about her nose job had gone undetected. Belligerently, she pulled out her white lace nightgown. "Here Mama, is this white enough?" She knew as soon as she spit out the words she had only fueled Mama's flames. The old woman began to wag her finger again. Oh no, Monica thought, here it comes. She prepared for another verbal onslaught.

"You thinka I don't know thatsa not you reala nose? Mama knows. Why you go anda change it? Does my Frankie know what you looka like before? Anda here, takea onea my flannel nightagowns and you be lots a warmer. Aspecially thata you sick." Mama handed her a well-worn thick flannel gown.

Monica ground her teeth. Of course Frankie didn't know what she looked like before. She had never even shown him a picture. She hated her old nose, besides, she had to have it done. She couldn't breathe well before, and that's exactly what she told Mama between fits of sneezing and wheezing.

"Anda now you cana breathe? Looka at you! You shoulda eat more then you woulda match you real nose. And, putta that gown ona. Isa onea my favorites. Everybody buy a olda lady nightagowns. They thinka all I do isa sleep."

Monica wanted to scream for Frankie, but she knew he was probably in the kitchen stuffing his face with meatballs and bread and catching up on family gossip with his cousin Rosalie. She touched her nose. She liked it and besides, all her girlfriends had their noses done before college. Mama was quiet for a moment. She was curiously rubbing her own large nose and then touched Monica's nose feeling it for reality. Soon the finger began to wag.

"You know, Frankie, hesa gotta biga nose anda alla you babies gonna have a biga noses, even ifa you do livea wherea alla the kids, they gotta little noses and blonde hair." Mama was pleased with her deduction.

That did it. Monica was furious. Who did Mama think she was, telling Monica her children would have big noses. The nerve of that woman! Still rummaging through her suitcase, Monica realized she had forgotten her hot rollers. She knew she hadn't had a touch-up in weeks, and she really needed them to get her hair just right to conceal the roots.

"Where are my hot rollers?" She screamed to no one in particular. "What in God's name am I going to do with my hair?" Unfortunately, Monica's outburst turned Mama's attention from her own nose to Monica's scalp.

"You hair, I knowa that's not you real color. I'ma no shtupeed. Doesa my Frankie know whata you really looka like?"

Monica began to ring her hands in despair. This old woman didn't miss a trick. She felt Mama's gaze travel up and down her root line and wished she had found the time for a touch up before they had left for skiing. She vowed never again to be so unprepared or allow herself to be so picked apart. Now Mama knew this wasn't her real hair color, or her original nose. Next, she'd be wanting to know where she had her teeth capped. Monica unwittingly looked in the mirror and forced a wide grin, observing her dentistry. Mama began her hearty laugh.

"What's so funny?" Monica demanded.

"You maka me think of Grandpa Chico. Hesa the only onea in the family who hada somethinga that was notta his. He hada falsa teeth and, you aska Frankie, he taka them out ana go chop, chop, chop. 'I'ma gonna get you.'" Mama was heaving with laughter.

Monica didn't know whether to laugh or cry, but the mention of teeth made her blush with embarrassment and jump to the defense without being further baited.

"These are my teeth. They're just capped! Very expensively, I might add."

Monica was shocked to hear the words she had just uttered. Mama seemed to be examining her teeth from every conceivable angle. She pinched her lips shut, and sat down on the bed, exhausted even beyond calling for Frankie's help. A tear or two started to trickle down her face. Mama, for all her frankness, had a tender heart and could not bear to see anyone cry. She waddled over to Monica and sat down on the bed beside her. For a moment the two women sat side by side, each lost in her own thoughts, Monica feeling dejected and Mama thinking how best to console her.

Mama's face suddenly lit up. "Herea now, we gonna sleepa in here tonight and I'ma gonna put ona my nightagown." Slowly, Mama unbuttoned the front of her housedress. Monica gasped, but Mama quickly assured her it was all right.

"You seea today they makea everything lika new. I betta if I wasa young now, I woulda had thema make a new breast, but years ago they no doa these things. But it wasn't aso bad. I feeda six kids witha one breast, but today, yes, I would even tella the doctor to makea an new one."

Monica had become very pale and quiet as she watched Mama slip into her nightgown.

"Hey, smile. It'sa not so bad. I'ma live a good life. It'sa not so bad you sleepa in here with me tonight. I sleepa alona for thirty years witha one breast and no teeth."

Monica was now sobbing openly. Sure she slept alone, the poor thing. She tried to dry her sniffles.

"Didn't you ever get lonely?" Monica asked Mama with a new compassion in her voice.

"Whata ya mean lonely? I raise all sixa of my children and somea therea children, too. I cooka anda I clean anda I sew theira clothes and they all still come to see me. They alla love Mama." Mama was beaming euphorically.

Monica looked at Mama through tear stained contact lenses, praying secretly that she would not have to take them out. God it sounded so sweet and sentimental a life, but how exhausting.

Mama wrapped her arms around Monica. "I hopea you anda Frankie havea many bambini anda then you seea what I mean."

"Oh no, Mama, Frankie and I want only two children, and we will probably have an au pair."

Mama was thinking. "I knowa today they canna helpa you do thata too, only have a few kids, but what'sa this au pair, che dice, au pair?"

"Why that's someone who lives with you and cooks and cleans and takes care of the children." Monica was pleased now that she and Mama were having a real conversation.

Mama got up beaming. "You no needa an au pair. I comma anda live with you anda Frankie and takea care ofa the bambini and I canna cooka too, maybe no clean."

Oh no, what had she started? Monica laughed while her mind raced, trying to come up with an answer. "No, Mama, an au pair is hired help, not a relative who comes to help out with the babies. Many young families have them."

"That's so sad. They gotta no family anda they gotta pay people to helpa them, but you anda Frankie, you got Mama. Maybe ifa some people need it'sa OK." Mama started laughing till tears were coming to the corners of her eyes.

"What's so funny?" Monica asked, caught up in the closeness she was experiencing with Mama.

"I'ma justa thinking. Whena Grandpa Chico died, therea was thisa man nameda Stanley who comma around, but I tella him getta the hell outa here. I know what you want. I gotta six kids. I don't needa no man. Now I know what I needed, an au pair. Thatsa what I needed." Suddenly Mama's laughter stopped and she became very serious. "Hey, buta will you kids love the au pair lika Frankie loves me?"

Monica just looked lovingly at Mama. Things were so different now. It was a good question, but how could she begin to explain. She glanced down to see one of the cats snuggled on Mama's lap. She patted its pink little nose, while the cat purred its acceptance.

"Achoo," she roared as a gigantic sneeze raced through her body. "Oh shit!" She screamed, as she jumped off the bed breaking a nail. "I've just broken another tip."

"Tip, che dice, tippa? Thosa notta you nails either." Mama was up inspecting her hands.

Just then, as if on cue, Frankie strolled happily into the bedroom. He grasped the two women in one enormous bear hug and urged them to come down and eat. They both looked up at him adoringly and smiled.

# Five O'clock World

A white fluffy polar bear doesn't belong in the sky, spreading her front paws like a swimmer, pointing her nose to heaven, carrying her cubs on her back. A daydream perhaps, but that's what Sarah saw in the guiltless blue sky above her on this balmy April morning. Daydreaming, and not paying enough attention to her driving, she watched the bear dissipate into feathery wisps of cirrus clouds, much more appropriate to the scenery on this mild spring day. Just like that, the cumulus vision of the polar bear disappeared into the warm air.

Sarah didn't like leaving her lakefront home in Mannington Meadows today. She felt uneasy. She had stood, for what seemed like hours, in front of her mirror, angling her head, this way and that, to catch a glimpse of her hair, hoping her dark roots didn't show. It was time to have them touched up. She liked her dark brunette hair frosted. It covered the gray she was not yet ready to acknowledge. Finally settling on what she was convinced looked like a very sophisticated upsweep, she turned sideways to view her profile. At thirty-six, her body was still hard and sleek, but she had to work harder at it, four times a week at the gym, sometimes maybe five. She wondered to herself, as she surveyed her body, what she would look like pregnant. She snickered at this persistent thought. There were not even any serious men in her life right now. Her career kept her in the office for long hours, but there had been that chance . . . She shook her head hoping to dispel the sudden discomfort that always stood lurking, ready to enter her day. She was too busy to think. So much time had already passed. She let her silk dress slip down over her head and watched as the lines of designer perfection fell softly around her slender frame. Each carefully purchased accessory stood ready and waiting to complete the desired look.

Driving long distances alone used to bother her, but now she enjoyed the solitude. It gave her time to think, time to go over her cases in her mind, to envision the juries. As she watched the gentle hills and manicured lawns slip past her, she felt exposed and vulnerable, especially on a day like today. Funerals were not high on her list of priorities. She usually avoided them like guilty clients, but this one was different. When she heard of Uncle Max's death, something deep urged her to go back to her hometown.

Going back home always made Sarah uncomfortable. She could not even think of what her life would have been had she not escaped after college. Determined to go to law school, she had made it. She was a success. Of course, there had been choices along the way. Most days she found them easy to accept, but as she grew older, she often wondered what her child would have looked like, especially when she thought about her high school boyfriend, Rob, and his family. What was the sense of looking back; she had no regrets. Thank God she wasn't smothered in a boring 9 to 5 existence. Moving far away from the blue-collar neighborhood of Passaic, where all her personal memories were stored, was the best thing she could have done. It distanced her. She was now a lawyer, living in a prestigious lakefront community. *Way to go, Sarah*, she beamed.

Passaic, the city where she grew up, like the mill industry that it was built upon, lay in a curious state of confused deterioration. Closed mills lined the river, the river whose brown-brackish water sludged a path through the town. Once Sarah's father had told her stories about fishing and swimming in that river when he was a boy, but there were no fish there anymore. Industry's fine dust had polluted the river and the lungs of many of the townsfolk, including her father and now her uncle Max, leaving only widows in its wake. It was there, along that river, she had played in the park, prayed in the Catholic Church and dreamt of a better life.

As she drove on, Sarah remembered her old neighborhood as an unchanging bustling community of new immigrants. Hard working blue collar men and women put in long hard days to make sure their children would have a better chance, a college education and more, much more than they did. Pride was evident in the glistening window trim, painted every year, on bright aluminum-sided houses. Postage-stamp-sized lawns were clipped and bordered with forsythia and geraniums. Religious statues smiled benevolently, with arms outstretched, welcoming the weary home. The factories had closed down years ago, the parent companies relocating, confiscating funds, denying pensions to the dedicated men who had struggled there for over twenty years. But some things had not changed. Pride was precious. Widows clung to their Social Security checks, and the few healthy remaining men tended the lawns and repainted the trim on the houses. The factories, with their broken windows, still sat on the banks of the river, staring gloomily into its depth and dominating the entire landscape.

She parked in front of the funeral parlor and looked into the rearview mirror, checking her makeup. She wondered if Rob would be there with his family. He had adored her Uncle Max as much as she did. They had all grown up on the same street across from the river. She entered quietly. Sarah knew the recitation of the rosary was about to begin. The parish priest had already started speaking to the mourners, so she sat down in the back row on one of the velvet-cushioned chairs.

The priest was somewhere in the middle of his eulogy. "And who is wise?" Sarah heard him say. "Why, he who sees what is born. He who can look at the seed and envision the tree. Max was a wise man, a man who never lost sight of the true purpose of his existence. Though he never amassed many physical possessions, the gentle graying man in the first pew every Sunday quietly commanded the love and respect of all who knew him. His kind and noble ways lead me to believe that he has known God and is now home."

Sarah looked around the funeral parlor and considered herself lucky to be seated. People were now standing along the walls, many of them in tears, deeply moved by the eulogy and their love of Max. Flowers filled the room, stacked side by side, among all the mourners. All heads were bent in prayer, remembering Max. Sarah tried to pray, but she felt she had forgotten how. The only words passing through her lips were, "I love you, Uncle Max." It became her own private litany as she fought back tears.

The stuffy air was filled with the scent of gladiolus and incense. The long drive had made her lethargic, and as the ornately garbed priests circled the casket, chanting and dispensing incense, the pomp and ceremony of the service began to make her drowsy. The incense began to inflame her allergies, and the pollen from the tall flower arrangements caused tears to blur her vision. She remembered Uncle Max as a tall man, an avid hiker, a gentle giant who couldn't wait for weekends to take his sons for long walks to the park or on trips to the mountains, a book of poetry in one hand and his journal in the other. How odd that a man who so loved the outdoors should now be surrounded by flowers on metal stands and lie dressed in a suit for eternity.

Sarah focused on the white gladioli, not willing to look at her uncle. They seemed to gently float up to the ceiling, becoming one with the drifting April clouds outside. Their metal stands grew strong and rugged and became the trees of her youth. A glen in a forest grew around the casket, and Uncle Max held her hand as her Daddy kissed her bruised knee, promising he would make it all better.

"Don't cry, sweetie," Daddy would say to her. "You're Daddy's big girl, be brave."

She still refused to cry. She didn't cry at her Daddy's funeral and she was not going to cry now. Daddy never knew about her abortion. She had confided only in Uncle Max. He had quietly pleaded with her to at least think it through. But she had her dreams. Sarah was determined to let nothing interfere with her plans for college and law school, not even the child she would have named Bobby.

"Sarah? Hi, how are you? Are you OK? You looked so lost in your own thoughts. I hated to disturb you."

Jolted back to reality, Sarah was now very much aware that the services were over and the onslaught of scattered relatives would be coming to say hello. She wanted to escape. She felt trapped by her cousin Jenny's presence. Jenny was overweight and pregnant again. She had married Rob, who now had to hold down two jobs just to make ends meet. Time was at a standstill here. No one had any aspirations. They all lived for that five o'clock whistle, the time to go home to their families.

"Oh, Hi Jenny, congratulations. I hear it's a boy again this time. Rob must be thrilled. Pretty soon he'll have his own basketball team." Sarah began to fidget with the pearls around her neck. "My allergies have been awful this year," Sarah said as she rummaged through her purse, looking for a tissue. "I think the antihistamine I took must have made me sleepy. I was starting to doze off. It's been so hectic lately. I really have to run back to the office. I don't think I can go to the cemetery. I felt obligated to come to the funeral. You know how it is with family stuff."

"I sure do," said Jenny, patting her stomach. "Here, say hello to the boys. Craig, Mike, Joe, this is Sarah, your cousin. She's a lawyer in Trenton." Jenny rumpled each boy's pale downy hair, ready to burst with joy. Happiness seeped out of every chubby pore.

"I've really got to go now, Jenny. If you're ever in the area, please look me up. The boys would love the lake house." Sarah turned, fleeing the room before anyone else could approach her. Jenny looked after her for a moment, and then felt the comforting embrace of her husband's arms around her growing middle.

"She looks wonderful, doesn't she? But so tense." As she leaned her body against Rob, Jenny sighed, smiled and looked up at her adoring husband.

Sarah raced to her car, determined to get back home as quickly as possible. "Damn these allergies," she screamed and sniffed to no one in particular. But she couldn't head home yet. She drove to the old abandoned factory and parked the car. She got out and stood in the same spot where she and her cousins had impatiently waited for her Dad and Uncle Max to come out of the factory every day and take them on their coveted trip to the park. She looked across the street and decided to walk. Her high heels felt wrong and uncomfortable, but she kept walking with more determination as she realized where she was headed. The park looked open. The bicycles were all lined up, gleaming with delight after a long winter storage. Children's laughter filled the air. There was not a coat or sweater that hadn't been flung to the wind. The tall oak tree by the pond still stood solidly, stretching its long arms up into the heavens. It was full of eager little tree climbers testing its newest limbs. Sarah squinted her eyes and looked upward. The branches on which she had learned to climb must be way up there by now. The swings were full, teasing the warm breezes, enticing them to stay. The slide kept whisking its playful cargo to a happy communion with the soft earth.

Sarah looked over in the other direction and could see the top of the ever-looming factory. She wondered where all the dads and uncles of these children now worked. She heard one boy crying on the basketball court, moaning at the stubborn pavement that had been unwilling to budge. The black asphalt had begun its spring tally of skinned shins and elbows. The court was filled with bouncing boys eagerly testing their newly acquired inches. The park seemed segregated by sex. The girls were off in another direction, flipping and twirling and springing the cold metal gymnastic bars back to life. School papers were manufactured hastily into paper gliders, while books flew open in the warm breezes, scattering loose papers into this sea of youth. Sarah watched quietly for a very long time, and then went over to the tall oak and touched the heavy bark. Suddenly feeling very exhausted, she sat down under it, leaning her weight against its trunk. Time seemed to go in slow motion. She watched a kite being brought down after its grand debut and knew that it must be getting close to supper hour. The young bodies that had seemed to fill the air with gravity-defying feats all drifted home. Two boys in a tangled wrestling skirmish giggled as their mothers finally came and pulled them apart. A puppy snapped up a long-ago discarded mitten and ran after the group.

With her perfectly manicured hands, Sarah began to smooth her wrinkled, peach-toned, silk dress. The fine dust of the city had mixed with the fresh green pollen, creating a mixture that Sarah thought was uniquely revealing. She traced her finger through this dust on her dress and marveled at the course her life had taken. A warm breeze blew her skirt and hair around her with the promise of spring. For that's what spring is, Sarah thought, a promise. A promise of summer and fall and winter, a promise of life. Sarah kept tracing her finger in the dust, watching as it became moist, teardrops now washing away the pollen. As she observed her tears spreading stains into the silk, she cried and she cried and she cried. "Damn these allergies," she screamed, as she finally wept for Bobby.

## Angel's Choice

There is a little known fact down there on earth, one we Christmas tree angels have kept secret for quite sometime. Once upon a long time ago, Christmas tree angels were handmade cherished heirlooms. Families made us with painstaking details and treasured us for generations and generations. Then the world began to change and people became frazzled and hurried and fewer and fewer of us were made at home. Suddenly we were being mass-produced, first in small workshops, then in huge factories. Our wings were made separately from our halos and strangers who would probably never see us again put us together. They would never even recognize their finished angel.

So, we Christmas tree angels decided to form a union, unfortunately for our long suffering makers, much earlier than they ever did. We talked about our lack of humanity in the new industrial age and decided we had to make some changes. Much of our time was spent standing around looking angelic in store shop windows and on counters. We were picked over like any other merchandise and sometimes even dropped and broken. Gone were the days when we were lovingly created by hands that tenderly cared for us. It was decided, if we were to survive this new age, we should have some choice in the matter of where we were going to spend the rest of our lives. And so the tradition of angel's choice was born. I've lived in my home for over fifteen years, but I will always remember my first Christmas atop her tree. Every year she treasures the time we spend together as well as her moments with all the other ornaments. We wind her down the lane of memories, breezing through past Christmases until she is dreaming gently of future carols. But I'm jumping ahead of myself. Let me tell you how we met.

When our union made the rule governing choice in our destinies, we still had to abide by general angel regulations. It is forbidden for Christmas tree angels to talk out loud. We were permitted the customary language of all angels, talking directly to the heart, but we thought we needed something stronger. We decided to try this for one year and if it didn't work we would renegotiate with management, which sometimes took eons. Off we all went into various department stores and craft shops, hoping and waiting for that perfect person to come into our visions, someone who would fulfill our wants and desires and let us meet theirs. I was placed in a card store, not a bad location, but not one I would have preferred. I had entertained visions of being placed in Bergdorfs or Bloomingdales; after all I had a delicate porcelain face and thin gossamer wings, but as card stores go, this one was not bad. It was in a lovely Connecticut town, and I envisioned dreamy snow-covered scenes. I did get those snow-covered Christmases, but not in Connecticut. Again I am jumping ahead in my story, anxious for you to know my fate.

I sat in the store window for over a month. It was not until after Thanksgiving that people began to admire me and inquire as to how much I might cost. At first I felt cheap and merchandised, but I soon realized all the angels had price tags, assuring their makers were paid. My wings began to get a little dusty and my fair porcelain skin a little gray. What was an angel to do? I did not see one person who caught my eye or looked interesting enough to spend a lifetime in their company.

One day I was abruptly taken out of the window. A huge jolly Santa Claus was put in my place with winking eyes and a shaking belly. I was placed on a top shelf, too fragile to be left on the counter. Many people inquired about my price tag, but gasped and said I was much too expensive for an ornament. Ornament, what did they know about Christmas tree angels anyway?

One gray, cold, rainy night a horrible thing happened after the store closed. People were in there cleaning and a broom hit the shelf, toppling me from my pedestal. I fell with a crash, broke my wrist, bent my wings, messed my hair, and, worst of all, smashed the magic wand I held in my hand. The poor old man who knocked me down, gently placed me back on the shelf, vainly attempted to brighten me up, and swept away the broken pieces of my magic wand. I cried most of the night, knowing no one would want me now. Even if I spoke out loud and not directly to their hearts, mine was a hopeless case. I was marked down the next day and taken off the top shelf. From then on I was handled and mishandled, but no one even showed a remote interest in taking me home, and neither was there anyone I wanted to pursue. Then she walked in five days before Christmas.

Dinah was her name and she looked sad. I couldn't imagine what she was so worried about with Christmas right around the corner and snow beginning to fall outside. It was going to be just the kind of Christmas dreams are made of, if I could only find a home. I was so disappointed when she passed me by and went straight to the Chanukah cards. My luck, the first person I wanted to talk to, appeared not to believe in Christmas, but then she stopped and looked in my direction.

"Oh I love you, I love you," I whispered to Dinah's heart. "Take me home. Take me home, please!"

She picked me up with such reverence, I thought I would faint and not be able to carry on my conversation with her. I knew she had heard me. I was certain. She smoothed my hair, and wiped the dust off my cheeks revealing their rosy glow. I was radiant. She looked at the broken stick where I once held my magic wand and I could hear her heart contemplating many different issues. She was a deep one all right. She was worrying about everything. Her arm moved in the direction of putting me back on the shelf and I cried out, "NO," so loudly it broke angel regulations and could be heard out loud. She looked at me quizzically and I was sure she had heard. I was saved! She tucked me in her basket and walked over to the Chanukah decorations. She found a white ceramic Star of David and played with the idea of putting it on the tip of the stick that used to hold my magic wand. Suddenly I felt more magical than ever.

"Oh, yes, Oh, yes, take me home. I can be a truly non-denominational angel. I could bring peace and brotherhood to all. I can teach people to love, not to hate. I can be so much more than just another pretty face. Take me home, Dinah! Take me home. You are my destiny. It will work! I promise you it will work!" She really managed to bring out the best in me.

With my final plea to her heart I was quickly bought and paid for along with the Star of David and various Christmas and Chanukah cards. I learned on the ride home all about her. She had married her childhood sweetheart and had two grown children. Her husband had died years ago and she was terrified of the future. Christmas in Vermont was not the same without him. I was the reassurance she needed. When she placed me on the top of her Christmas tree, with the Star of David firmly attached to the tip of my wand, I felt the magic. I realized that Vermont would be my new home, and this family was mine.

Now I watch Dinah light Christmas candles beside the Menorah as she welcomes guests and family from every religion, in every season, to her Vermont home. I assure them love is the only answer, as I stand atop her tree proudly proclaiming my message. So the next time you pass a Christmas tree angel and she cries out to you with pleading eyes, stop and think. Maybe, she is exercising her Angel's right to choose and maybe, just maybe, she will change your life forever.

# And On The Third Day

*Let each new temple, nobler than the last,*
*Shut thee from heaven with a dome more vast,*
*Till thou at length are free.*
*Leaving thine outgrown shell by life's unresting sea!*
Oliver Wendell Holmes

The green hospital gown was soft and not entirely uncomfortable. The discomfort was deeper. It came from the escalating terror in her soul. Two hours ago, she had dutifully swallowed a little radioactive pill. Now she would have to lie silently, lie still, beneath this huge hovering cone, while it traced the active particles journeying through her body. This enormous mechanical wonder would search out and pinpoint the body snatchers that were once again slowly threatening to steal her life.

Relax and fight this, she kept repeating to herself. You've done it once before and you can do it again. You have total confidence in Dr. Everett.

Unfortunately, it was Dr. Judith Blair, Dr. Everett's new associate, who was administering the test. For some reason, she made Sherry very uneasy and Sherry had to fight to achieve tranquility. It was going to be a long morning.

At least the morning had started normally. Sherry had gotten up at the crack of dawn to feed her horses. Sean was still asleep, so she quietly slipped out of bed trying not to disturb him on his one day off. She had promised to wake him but instead gently kissed his forehead and watched him stretch and smile as if the kiss were part of a pleasant dream. Her thoughts, as well as the chill in the morning air, sent goose bumps up and down her flesh, and she hurried to put on her warm terry cloth robe. She thought she had this cancer thing beaten, but after seven years, it looked as if the invasion of cells that were determined to rob her of life had returned. As she slipped into her jeans and paddock boots, her heart seemed ready to burst. Her life was so full right now. Things were so near perfect. Wasn't that always the way? When you want to stop time, to relish the perfection, time threatens to do just that...stop.

As she made her way out to the barn, she walked through the hallway filled with her class photos. Though she and Sean had no children of their own, her many years of teaching had been fulfilling. She loved her job and couldn't imagine one that wasn't filled with children. How she enjoyed the freedom of summers off! She spent this time as Master of the Hounds, leading the foxhunts through the hills and valleys of the countryside with the authority of a huntress. In fact, that is what had first attracted Sean. He watched her gallop up the field behind his farm with her hair flying in the wind and thought he had laid his eyes on a goddess. It was the most sensual thing he had ever seen, and he stopped her to tell her so. Relieved that she was not going to be chastised for cutting across his private property, she smiled and told him riding was the most sensuous thing she ever did. After a few weeks of, now uncoincidental meetings, they began to see each other regularly. Soon they were inseparable.

She felt exhilarated as she led the pack of hounds, and experienced riders, over ditches and fences, through streams and wild terrain in pursuit of a fox they would allow to win. It had taken Sean many years to understand these long weekends away and the exuberant drinking and partying that followed the hunt. In the beginning, he would go everywhere with Sherry. She suspected that he was slightly jealous of all the male friends that accompanied her on these hunts. He also had a quiet aversion to alcohol that Sherry did not fully understand. She had never even seen him take one drink. His lips barely touched the glass of the toast on their wedding day. After a while, he stayed away from the long hunting weekends, obviously preferring the quiet solitude of his own farm. For some reason, Sherry thought, Sean seemed to live with the fear that she would someday leave him, yet she was completely devoted to their marriage and believed very strongly in fidelity.

The horses began to whinny and frolic as they saw Sherry approach. She filled their water buckets, added the sweet feed to their oats, and threw in several bales of hay. Jenny, her pet cat, sat on the split rail fence, regally surveying the whole scene; she gazed at the horses with absolute superiority. Sherry shook her head and laughed. The airs that cat put on. She was aloof and unfriendly to everyone but Sherry. She merely tolerated Sean. Sherry breathed deeply enjoying the scent of the barn and the cool crisp morning dew. It was right here she felt most at home. The smell of the damp earth blended with the smell of molasses and sweet oats, filling her with a much-needed sense of serenity. This was what life was all about.

Having finished her morning routine, she went back inside to shower and get ready. The horses would have to wait till much later to be ridden. She had to be at the hospital before noon. Sean was already up and making coffee.

"Don't you want me to go with you, Babe? I thought you were going to wake me up." Sean had put his arms around Sherry's waist, and he could feel his own heart anxiously beating against her back.

The old terror began to fill him. *Please God let her be all right*, he mumbled over and over to himself as he tenderly smothered the back of her neck with kisses and told her out loud that he was sure everything would turn out fine.

Sherry turned to face him and kissed the tip of his nose. "I'll be just fine, Sweetheart. I've been through all this before. I really prefer to go alone. I have to do it by myself. I hope Doctor Everett is there and not his new associate. There is something about her that makes me very uneasy. I don't know what it is. She really is the sweetest thing but...oh who knows, I'm being silly. I've really got to run. I'll be home as soon as I'm done. Don't worry, I love you."

Now she had to lie there while she watched Dr. Blair go through the mechanics of setting up this machine.

"Now don't move," Dr. Blair quietly commanded. "I know it will be hard to be perfectly still, but you'll have to stay in this position for the next twenty minutes." She positioned Sherry's head and neck and Sherry closed her eyelids, trying to shut out the bright lights. She also tried to close her mind to the occurring events and surprisingly found herself drifting into a semi-slumber.

The reality of the moment was fading fast. She moved her fingers slightly, touching her robes and felt the hard rough stone beneath her hand. Her incandescent white gown spread out in long folds over the altar upon which she dozed. The sounds of the guttural Mayan chantings and the smell of the burning incense had relaxed her. She was secure with the knowledge that the honor bestowed upon her was the greatest any young woman could attain in this lifetime. Her only regret was that she would miss her thirteen younger brothers and sisters, but they must be so proud of her at this moment. She loved all the little ones in the village and promised they would all meet again. She knew she would not even feel the plunge of the dagger when it came, releasing her into eternity to join the God Quetzalcoatl. The herbal potion that she had been given to drink after the purifying steam bath was beginning to take effect and her mood was positively euphoric. She would meet her God in ecstasy.

"Sherry, you can turn your head now," Dr. Blair interrupted. Sherry looked up, not quite sure where she was and smiled up at Dr. Blair. "You were wonderful. You never moved an inch. That will make these tests very easy to read. Now turn your head the other way, and we'll proceed with the other side."

The terror that Sherry felt had completely vanished. Now she felt strangely off balance. "I think I dozed off for a little while." She quietly turned her head, not wishing to fall into some inexplicable void.

Sherry closed her eyes again, and felt the silky folds of ribbon being wrapped around her young body. She was eager for the day to proceed. She would be carried down the river on a barge and laid to rest in the pyramid beside her beloved Akhenaton and her royal pet cat. They would all be united under the benevolent gaze of their God. Right now, her handmaidens were preparing all her favorite jewels to be brought with her into the afterworld. Two solid gold replicas of her cat would stand beside her tomb, guarding it for eternity. It broke her heart to witness one of her faithful servants pocket a tiny gold ring, an image of the crescent moon that should have gone with her. She would be certain never to trust her in the afterworld. The barge began to move as the cool wind picked up the currents.

Dr. Blair walked up to Sherry and watched her lying peacefully on her side. Most people fidgeted and always seemed on the verge of hysteria. Sherry was handling this extremely well. "OK, Sherry," Dr. Blair said quietly, feeling almost guilty for disturbing her. "We're almost half way through. Now all you have to do is lie on your back. These last scans won't take nearly as long."

Sherry rolled on her back, looked up at Dr. Blair dreamily, and smiled. That familiar feeling of uneasiness began to surface ever so slightly. She watched Dr. Blair write in her pad, and was sure she was making a note to test her blood work for drugs. Sherry knew that her calm manner always slightly unnerved Dr. Blair, but surprisingly, this made it easier to relax. Dr. Blair moved the cone and zeroed it into place. She watched as Sherry happily closed her eyes again and faded off into oblivion.

Sherry could feel the long folds of her gown now floating in the warm breeze off the Mediterranean Sea. All of her fellow Gods and Goddesses had come to see her carried off into the heavens. The full moon, her sign and symbol, glowed in the dark sky, beckoning her home to the land of her father, Jupiter. Her time with the mortals had been well spent. Roman warriors lined the entrance to the temple, waiting for the moon to be eclipsed. It was at that moment they would be assured their beloved Goddess was safely home. She clutched her bow and quiver of arrows proudly as she crossed the river boundary between the two worlds. Tears were in the eyes of the strongest of warriors; even the animals wept. They all vowed to follow her into eternity.

Sherry was not consciously aware of the cone being moved, and this time barely blinked her eyes. She felt slightly delirious but extremely content. It hovered and lowered above her stomach, and Dr. Blair was amazed at the stillness with which she lay. The soft whirring sound of the machine was one with the rushing meadow brook that careened through her beloved Gaelic village. The green hills of the countryside stretched out before her. The soft folds of her linen burial gown felt comforting. As were all the members of her family, she would be buried beneath the willow in the family plot alongside the meadow where the young colts were turned out every spring. It had been a tragic accident and she blamed herself. No longer able to tolerate her husband's drinking and temper tantrums, she had told him she was leaving him, this time for good, regardless of the consequences. She had saddled the stallion and galloped off with tears in her eyes. The rain beat unmercifully down upon the earth as Seamus watched helplessly, yelling after her in a drunken stupor. The fall, as her horse jumped the muddy slippery stonewall, was painless. Death came instantly with the break in her neck. Seamus was never the same again. Folks still called him the village drunk but he went through the remainder of his days in mourning, never once touching another drop of brew.

Sherry stretched ever so slightly to undo the crimp in her neck as Dr. Blair moved the cone down over her legs. "Now this is the last sequence. Let your hands lie down at your sides and relax and breathe deeply." Sherry never even bothered to open her eyes so lost was she in time and space.

As she put her hands down at her sides, she felt the warm moist earth in her fingertips. She looked around the cold dark cave and grunted. Bacca, the sleek black panther that had mothered her since her tribe abandoned her, licked her face and purred in return. The days were over when she would race through the jungle on her back. She was dying now, and would return to the earth right here in this cave that had been her home. As she closed her eyes for the last time, she envisioned the happy moments of flying through the forest clinging to Bacca's back, her hair flying wildly in the wind.

Dr. Blair moved the cone from atop Sherry and gazed at the serene look on her face. Her hair lay spread out on the hospital table around her face. She had apparently fallen asleep. "Sherry, you can wake up now. The tests are all over. Dr. Everett and I will go over the results with you tomorrow in the office."

Sherry opened her eyes and stared up at Dr. Blair. Dr. Blair's hand still rested on the cone. Sherry's calm frank stare appeared, for some unexplained reason, to make Dr. Blair very nervous.

"That's a lovely ring, doctor," Sherry said to her own amazement, since she rarely wore any jewelry herself. "What an interesting design of the moon. Where did you get it? It must have cost a fortune." Sherry watched Dr. Blair blush and become very uneasy. Sherry did not mean to embarrass her and she was angry with herself for being so rude. What had gotten into her?

Dr. Blair, not looking directly at Sherry, told her that it was a very old family heirloom. Sherry slid off the hospital table and ran her fingers through her long hair, pulling it back off her face. As she dressed, she decided that she would definitely seek another opinion, no matter what the results of the test. She had learned to follow her hunches, and Dr. Blair had the uncanny knack of making them both feel entirely uneasy. She was surprised to find Sean waiting in the lobby below. The look of delight and relief on his face when he spotted her made her heart leap with pride. God, she really did love him.

"Hi Sweetheart. How'd it go?" he tried to mumble under her kisses. For some reason, Sherry felt ecstatic, confident and very, very hungry. She was dying for a pizza. She threw her arms around his waist and they walked out into the twilight together.

"It was a long day, Sean, but I know everything will be all right. Let's go and grab something to eat. I'm starved. I feel like I haven't eaten in ages and I'm probably glowing in the dark. Look, there's the first star. Make a wish."

Sean looked up at the star as it twinkled a Morse code message of universal proportions meant only for them. He put his arm around Sherry's waist. "I wish, I may," he said. "I wish I might...."

# Red Geraniums

Gloria was finally comfortable leaving psychoanalysis for a five-week hiatus when her past sat down in her path. All her associates at work believed she led an ideal life. Only Gloria knew what hard work it had been to keep up that facade. She had learned to love her husband, despite his air of indifference. According to her analyst, it was either that or she had to make up her mind to leave him; changing him was out of the question. That, Gloria had finally accepted, was up to her husband and his analyst. So, here she was childless on the eve of her 40th birthday, her husband away on a gambling junket to Atlantic City, and her analyst out of town for the month of August. It all converged with three rings from the phone.

"Hello," Gloria mumbled into the receiver.

"What's with the death voice, Gloria? It's me, Ginger. Boy have I got some news for you."

What was she going to do? Her sister, Ginger, rattled on and on. Seems their parents had just decided to put their house up for sale and move out of state. Gloria sat down and took several deep breaths. Her analyst said this would help in times of stress, but her heart beat wildly. Ginger couldn't understand the silence on the other end of the line.

"Gloria, are you still there? Speak to me! Gloria, Gloria?"

Finally Gloria pulled herself together enough to answer Ginger with some semblance of sanity.

"Ginger?" She spoke so softly she almost could not be heard. "I just didn't expect this. Why didn't anyone tell me?"

"I am telling you, Gloria. I just found out this morning. Mom is calling the boys, probably as we speak. They want us to go through the house and see if there is anything we want. God knows I've got all sorts of stuff stashed there, old high school yearbooks, tons of memorabilia. I want it, but can't imagine where I'll put it all now that I'm living in this tiny condo. Divorce is the pits, you know. You're smart to hang on to Bud even though he's such a shit sometimes. I barely have room for my necessities and myself in this dump. Isn't it just like Mom and Dad to not say anything until they've reached a final decision? And guess where they're moving, not even to Florida, where it would be great to visit, but Upstate New York. Who the hell ever heard of retirees moving to Poukeepsie? Gloria, Gloria are you still there?"

Sitting on the edge of the bed with the phone cradled in her lap, Gloria hung her head between her legs. Her long red hair, the color of golden-red poppies, cascaded to the floor. She heard her sister's words but her mind raced, spinning through every room of the house her parents were about to sell. She could smell the bittersweet aroma of the red geraniums her father had tended with such care and the constant smell of alcohol on his breath. Once again she was a child, alone and afraid in her pink and white bedroom. She put the phone to her ear and whispered, "Where are they?"

"What?" Ginger, stammered. "Where are who? I was just going to hang up. Where are you?"

"Mom and Dad, where are they? Why didn't they tell me?"

"Geez, Gloria, why should they tell you? You and Mom have been pretty distant these last few months. Dammit! Bud, your vagabond husband, wasn't even over the house for Mother's Day. Even on Mother's Day he has to go to the casino? Come on Gloria, what happened? Did he have words with Mom and Dad?"

"No! No! I begged him not to, not yet, but I told him everything I could."

"What are you talking about, Gloria. You're not making any sense. You begged him not to fight with Mom and Dad for the time being. Well, I don't know what's up with you two, but I'm going over to the house tomorrow to start sorting through some of the stuff. Are you coming with me?"

"Where are they?"

"Who, Mom and Dad? They've gone upstate for the closing on the new house. They've really had this planned for some time."

"I'll be there at twelve tomorrow," Gloria stammered. "Do you have a key?"

"Of course. Don't you?"

"No, I gave it back."

"Why?"

"Twelve o'clock tomorrow, Ginger. I'll be there. Please don't be late."

"OK. Want to grab lunch first? I haven't seen much of you since you went back to school. Do your really think you want to be a psychoanalyst? Yuk, listening to other people's problems all day. You should start with a case study of our family."

"I just might," Gloria muttered. "I have to go now. I'll see you tomorrow at twelve. Maybe we'll eat lunch after. We'll see. Ginger, I love you."

"I love you too, nut case. See ya tomorrow."

Gloria hung up the phone and began to sob. Unleashed, her sobs had no reason to stop. Bud would not be home and her classes were over. She beat the pillow; she continued to cry; her eyes became puffy and swollen; she looked in the mirror and wished she were dead. She wanted to forget, to pretend she hadn't started analysis; pretend the past had never happened; pretend she wasn't burdened. She had pretended too long. She had begun to face the facts and now this. It was all happening too quickly. She doubted if she was ready. She wanted more time. She wished her analyst was in town but fantasized that she was probably vacationing somewhere exotic with the hope of never seeing her pathetic patient, Gloria, again.

"Gloria you are a mess!" She shouted out loud to herself. "Get yourself together!" There, that was better.

Gloria checked her list of things to do for today. The cleaning lady was sick and wouldn't be here tomorrow so she started to clean. With frenzied energy, she polished all her furniture, scrubbed every floor and made her bathrooms glisten. Bud would be home tomorrow night and she wanted everything to appear normal. He was always furious whenever he saw her upset. She wanted no confrontations. She also had to find time to bake the birthday cake she had promised a friend and to help out in the restaurant Bud owned. Bud counted on her when he was out of town on one of his junkets. By the time she fell asleep, she was exhausted. Exhaustion left her no time to think, no time to try and figure out who she really was or what she really wanted in life. Depending more and more on her therapy sessions, flights of fancy and daydreaming occurred only on Monday nights with her therapist.

Actually her analyst was starting to unnerve her. "Let's talk about you," she kept repeating. Gloria could summon no words then. That question always left her searching for a phantom. Wasn't it enough that she was going to school? That was a life. Soon she would be a therapist herself. She was much happier talking about and caring for others. They, all the others, took so much of her time there was little time left to confront her own dilemmas and fears. Tomorrow she would meet Ginger and then? Who knew what would happen then?

She met Ginger promptly at noon. It had taken her almost two hours to shower, dress and put on her makeup. She wanted to look ready, mature, in control, but inside she shook like a terrified child. She checked her mirror twelve times before finally venturing out of the house. She raced out knowing she would be at least fifteen minutes late. Ginger would understand. Gloria was always late. She never felt all put together.

"Hey, Gloria, you look great. How do you like my new haircut?"

Gloria looked blankly at her sister's hair. Once as long and luxurious as hers, it now stood, sprayed, gelled or what have you, into ultra-short spiky protrusions around her face. In the sunlight, her head looked like a copper penny struck by lightening.

Ginger continued, "I guess we're having lunch. Wait until you see the pile of shit mom has piled up in the living room. She brought every thing up from the basement and down from the attic and said if we don't take it, it all goes to Goodwill. Could you imagine she would send all our old yearbooks to Goodwill?"

They were standing in the back sunroom. The sunlight sparkled through the glass windows highlighting her father's red geraniums. Red geraniums. That's even what he affectionately called his girls. The red flowers craned their necks up against the plate glass begging for the warmth of the sun. Gloria turned away in disgust. Everything here looked so perfect. She sat down on the rattan rocker and began to take deep breaths. Rocking maniacally back and forth, she clutched her stomach. The waves of nausea panicked her.

"Hey, Gloria! What's wrong? Are you OK? I'll miss this place too but not that much."

Ginger hugged her older sister's shoulders and the rocking subsided.

"This is not the way I wanted to tell you Ginger. I wanted a chance to confront Dad. I've already told Mom and she doesn't believe me. I wanted to close this chapter in my life. I wanted to walk out of this house with my head up high. It was never my fault. In the end I did it to protect you."

"What are you talking about, Gloria. Boy, you must have had some fight with Mom and Dad, but it will pass. It always does."

"This won't pass, Ginger. I told Mom everything."

"You told Mom what?"

"Ginger, I, I, can't deal with this. Telling Mom was the hardest thing I have ever done in my life and now she won't even speak to me. I'm the reason they're moving away."

Gloria got up and started to pace, running her fingers through her long red hair. She had let it grow after years of keeping it cut short and tight like a little boy. Almost like Ginger wore hers now, but more subdued. Something about the tactile sensation of her fingers on her hair made her tears stop and she began to bite her lip. Pacing faster and faster, she walked over to the geraniums and started snapping their blossoms off one by one.

"There! There! I hate you! I hate you! You stole my childhood. Bastard! Bastard! Bastard! Bastard!" she screamed at each blossom until they all lay lifeless on the floor.

"Gloria, are you mad?" Ginger jumped up. "Mom and Dad will kill us. The broker has to show the house and those plants added a great touch, besides; Dad loved them. They were special to him."

"So was I special to him, Ginger." Grabbing the long box of planted geraniums, Gloria ripped it away from its place of honor and dumped the remaining plants and soil all over the rug. Stomping on the plants and dirt, she began to scream, "That's how special I was to him Ginger! So special that he fucked up my life! Oh Ginger, I wanted to confront him so many times. I just wasn't ready." Gloria sat on the floor in the dirt and began to sob.

Ginger sat beside her, aware something terrible was taking place. Gloria was speaking about things that she knew would change their lives forever.

"Gloria, tell me what's going on. I'm sure Mom and Dad didn't mean to hurt you."

"It went on for six years, Ginger, from the time I was ten, until I was sixteen and left home with Bud. He fucked me, Ginger, and he made me keep silent! He said if I didn't, he would kill Rusty. You know how I loved that dog. As I got older he said if I didn't let him into my bed he would go into your room. I hated him and I loved him and now, and now, I don't know what I feel."

Ginger fell into a deep silence as she sat on the floor and began to hold and rock her big sister.

The house stood silent, still and calm.

"I know honey. I know." Ginger began to murmur. "I know, honey. I know."

"Oh Ginger, I didn't want to hurt anybody."

"I know. I know, Honey," Ginger continued in a soothing voice. She left her sister's side and lifted the top of the bench where her parents kept their tools. She grabbed a hammer and threw it against the plate glass window, smattering it into millions of tiny crystalline pieces that fell in perpetual slow motion amidst the conquered geraniums.

Gloria, in complete shock, stared at her sister. Blood was dripping from her face where a piece of flying glass had nicked her cheek but she felt suddenly serene. A smile appeared on her lips surprising her and then she began to laugh and cry at the same time.

Ginger picked up a tissue, dabbed at Gloria's cheek and muttered, "See, not much damage at all. Nothing that won't heal in a few days. Come on, let's get the hell out of here and have lunch. I think we have a lot to talk about. I always hated those red geraniums too."

## Boys Will Be Boys

Darkness descends swiftly by the end of November; so at 5:30, when the station wagon, loaded with Thanksgiving leftovers, died in the fast lane on the Interstate, the sky had already blackened. Stephanie, driving with two sleeping passengers, tried not to panic, allowing the car to coast to a stop beside the guardrail. Her fiancé, David, asleep in the passenger seat, rubbed his eyes. Her sister, Maggie, awakened by the cessation of motion, stretched in the back seat.

"Quick trip," she murmured. "I slept the whole way. Haven't opened my eyes since we left home." Suddenly wide awake, Maggie had her hand on the door handle, ready to bound out of the car into the path of an oncoming tractor-trailer.

"Whoa, Maggie, settle down. We're not there yet. We're lucky to be alive. The damn car stopped dead. Lost the lights, heater, everything and we're in the middle of nowhere. Thank God we were able to coast to the side of the road."

"Shit," Maggie mumbled. "It's black as coal out there, not even a light in the distance. Wake up your damn fiancé."

"I am up, smart ass," David yawned. "What's the deal?"

"The deal is we're stopped. No power at all."

"Are you sure you have gas? Did you try the car phone, Stephanie?"

"David, of course I checked the gas. And, excuse me. How do you expect the car phone to work? I just said there is no power. Nothing."

"Are you two starting one of your famous arguments now? Maybe someone should just get out and check under the hood?"

"And should that someone be me?" David snidely remarked, putting on his cashmere gloves. He got out of the car, slammed the door and lifted the hood.

"I'm sure David won't even find the engine," Maggie chided her sister. "And, what the hell is he going to do with those fancy gloves on?"

"Oh, he'll pretend he knows every spark plug. He needs to feel in control; besides, when it comes to anything mechanical, I'm an idiot. I always acquiesce. David's better with machinery. No need to communicate. I distrust anything that won't talk to me."

"Well that would include David. You acquiesce to everything he says. I still can't believe...."

David stomped back into the passenger seat, interrupting their talk.

"I haven't a clue," he grumbled, "and it was impossible without a flashlight. Haven't I asked you a thousand times to put one in the glove compartment?"

"Grudgingly admitting defeat, are we? Didn't have a clue, did ya David?"

"What's that sign up ahead?" Stephanie asked, trying to diffuse the tension between David and her sister.

"Who knows? I can barely see you guys," Maggie yawned, rubbing her eyes, re-entering the world of the living.

They all shivered as the car shook with the force of two tractor-trailers coming within inches of their unlit station wagon.

"Well, at least we won't starve or freeze. This Subaru wagon is well equipped. A regular suburban defense system. Food, clothing, shelter. What else do we need?"

"A new car, Stephanie. Maybe David should hop over the guard-rail and see what's beyond the trees."

"Beyond what trees?" David asked, annoyed with this suggested inconvenience. "You can't see a thing in that direction, except for a few lights in the distance."

"Wimp!" Maggie hissed, while Stephanie grinned secretly in the dark.

"All right, you two. I'm going. I've got to take a leak anyway."

Stephanie and Maggie watched David quickly disappear after climbing over the low rail. They stared at the empty space, too terrified to get out and wave down a truck for help, or worse yet, follow David into blackness.

"Why do you stay with that arrogant creep, Stephanie? Especially since…. I can't believe you went ahead with that abortion."

"Maggie, stop. We said we'd never bring it up."

"But, you said that was it. It was over between you two after that, and you're still with the creep."

Stephanie opened the car door and walked up to the rail. Maggie followed right behind her.

"I'm sorry, Steph, but every time he hurts you, you go back for more. Look, there's a sign up ahead. Let's just push the car down there. At least we'll know where we are."

Stephanie was wiping tears from her cheek, when they heard David groan. He was crawling up the side of a steep hill, the frantic mooing of cows competing with his curses and the sound of traffic.

"David, are you OK? Maggie and I were about to go looking for you," Stephanie fibbed.

"Actually," Maggie added, "we decided to push the car down to that barely discernible road sign, in case you were hurt, David, or better yet, missing."

"Thanks a lot for the sarcasm, Maggie. I'm not hurt, but my new Ferragamos are covered in cow manure. I'm not going back down there to look for help. Let me try to start the car."

David got into the driver's seat, pressing and clicking every button and knob.

"Damn, nothing works. I really wrenched my back out there. Why don't you girls get out and push. I'll steer."

"What?" they screamed. "You expect us to push?"

"You know how bad my back is. It's mostly down hill to that sign, anyway."

Stephanie and Maggie pushed. David steered.

"God forbid David should decide to get his hands dirty," Maggie blistered. "I'm thrilled he's covered in cow shit. What you're still doing with that jerk is beyond me," Maggie railed at her sister. "Maybe we should just push the car off the side of the road."

"Hey, it's my car, Maggie. Besides, he'd sue us for damages if we didn't kill him."

"You're right about that, Steph. Hot shot Wall Street lawyer would sue his own grandmother. Asshole! Let me push. You shouldn't be doing this. It's too soon after...you know."

"Maggie, we promised not to talk about that. Ever!"

"Shit, Stephanie, who ever heard of a guy telling his fiancée he'll set a wedding date only if she aborts his child. He's such a jackass, and you go along...."

"Maggie, enough. Hey, is that what I think it is?"

An emergency call box appeared in the highway gloom like a religious vision.

David jumped out of the car and threw open the hood.

"Just in case any Good Samaritans finally pass," he crowed, again assuming control.

"One of you girls call. It's better if cops hear a woman's voice. Believe me, I know cops."

Maggie tried the call box, mumbling to her sister, "He knows cops, he knows diddly shit. Damn it! The Goddamn phone is dead!"

"Let's all get back in the car," Stephanie pleaded under the roar of over-bearing trucks. "It's not safe out here."


They waited and waited. It got darker and colder. Finally, a welcoming flashing red light pulled up behind them. Maggie and Stephanie were so elated, it could have been the second coming of Christ, the new Messiah arriving in a police car.

"It sure took them long enough," David scowled.

"Good evening Ma'am." The local officer smiled the sexiest molar-to-molar smile Stephanie had ever seen. "Having a bit of a problem here?"

"What the fuck does it look like?" David interjected from the passenger seat.

"Oh, I see you ladies have a gentleman with you. Well, I'm officer Toby Raye. Pleased to make your acquaintance, ladies. I'll just radio a tow truck driver, unless your gentleman friend there has a better idea."

"Oh, thank you so much," Stephanie meowed, pinching David's knee, hoping to keep his mouth shut.


The tow truck appeared, quickly.

"This is my cousin, Burt Raye," Officer Toby Raye beamed. "Best damn mechanic in these parts. Truth is, he's the only damn mechanic in these parts."

In the gleam of the tow truck's headlights, both Rayes laughed, slapping each other heartily on the back.

David mumbled under his breath, "Great, two fuckin' redneck cousins. Comedians, no less."

"Shut up," Maggie hissed softly, watching her sister smile at Officer Raye.

"That fella giving you any trouble Ma'am," the officer drawled.

"No sir. He was just remarking on how lovely it is that everyone was related. One big happy family. Nobody knows anybody in New York City."

"Seems to me he should learn a little about respect."

By now, David's knee was turning black and blue. Glumly, he decided to keep his mouth shut, and they all got out of the car.

Burt Raye hitched the station wagon to a large hook, started his engine and cranked the car up on to his flatbed truck.

"Now you all get in the police car with Officer Toby Raye. He knows the way to my shop."

Obediently, they did as they were told. David opened the front door on the passenger side of the police car.

"Why, I think it would be respectful if you let your wife sit up front, sir. Which one of these beauties is your wife, by the way?" Officer Toby Raye inquired, never taking his eyes off Stephanie.

"None of us. Thank God." Maggie smirked. "He's only been engaged to my sister for four years."

"Well, you don't say. Get in the back, sir. Let your little lady there come up front."

Stephanie quietly got out of the back seat, exchanging seats and dirty looks with David. She was certain Officer Toby Raye could hear her heart pounding. He was so damn gorgeous.


At Raye's Auto Body and Mechanic Shop, Burt looked under the hood. With an angelic smile, the burly mechanic told the trio the car required a major repair.

"The timing belt is broken, Ma'am. Not possible to fix it until Monday, when that Jap dealership opens upstate. But not to worry, ladies," he drawled, totally ignoring David. "I got me another brother, just up the road a-piece; he and his wife own the local pizza parlor, they do. Why don't you all mosey on down there and relax, enjoy dinner, while I make sure about the car."

David looked at his Rolex and then at Burt with disdain, distrusting anyone without a graduate school education. Stephanie could tell his low blood sugar was taking its toll. Soon he would be irritable and even more testy than normal, uncomfortable out of his oak-paneled office and court room surroundings.

"That's a fantastic idea," Stephanie offered before David could speak.

"What do we do with all the shit in the car?" Maggie whined.

"Well, I guess you dear folks should take it with you, since I'm going to close up the shop real quick, soon as I take a final look at your car. Let that there gentleman carry it over while I show you ladies to the restaurant. Follow me girls."

Maggie and Stephanie were led away by Burt. David sullenly schlepped the leftovers and overnight bags, uncharacteristically walking behind the group. As they turned the corner, Raye's Pizza Parlor came into view.

"I can't believe this is your brother, too," Stephanie giggled.

"Yes, Ma'am," Burt replied.

Maggie put her lips close to Stephanie's ear. "I think this is getting creepy, Steph."

"Shush. I think it's charming."

"I think you're nuts."


"Hi Betty. Take good care of these here folks. Fix them up one of Raye's special pizzas with the works. Oh, hi there, Clarence. Thought you was still up hunting. Ladies, this here is my brother Clarence and his wife Betty."

David entered the pizza parlor, flinging down their belongings in the corner.

"Something bothering that there fella?" Clarence asked.

"Na, just seems he got a chip on his fancy shoulder," Burt replied.

David looked at Betty and Clarence Raye behind the counter. He stared intently at the long fresh scratch on Clarence's face. Stephanie could see the lawyerly warning signals going off in his brain.

"Oh fuck it," she thought, suddenly wondering what she ever saw in the arrogant creep. "We'll see how hungry he really is."

Apparently, David was very hungry. He did not say a word. After looking at the well-traveled turkey leftovers in the corner, he asked if he could have a plain pizza, not a Raye's special.

"Something the matter with my special?" Clarence, the pizza brother, asked.

"I keep Kosher," David replied smugly.

"What's that mister? Are you a Catholic?" Clarence laughed at his own feigned ignorance.

"No," David snapped. "Ignorant baboon," he whispered, not too silently to Stephanie and her sister.

They ate their pizzas in silence. Soon after they finished eating, the thought began buzzing through everyone's brain that they might be stranded here. The pizza parlor closed at eleven, and even though it was only approaching nine, an element of doubt began to cloud their thoughts. Everything had been too easy. Stephanie opened her library book, and

Maggie flipped through a French fashion magazine, while David kept glancing at his watch and pacing. He walked over to the counter and picked up the local newspaper.

"Great! No business section. Hmm....Stephanie, Maggie, look at this. Nice little town in New Jersey we got stranded in." He walked over to the two sisters and plopped the newspaper down between them.

"What a gruesome murder," Stephanie's eyes filled with horror.

Maggie was busy studying the newspaper when a petite bubble of energy burst through the door.

"Where's the party who got stranded on the Interstate?"

"Surprise! Here we are," David answered sarcastically. "The only customers in this restaurant."

"Well," she said, "I'm Nanette Raye. My husband and I are the directors of Raye's Funeral Home. Burt told us you were in need of a car. We have an extra van you could borrow, and you can return it when Burt is finished fixing your car. Come with me and we'll make all the arrangements. And Mister, I'm used to being talked to like a lady."

Maggie and Stephanie felt the secret smile in Nanette's eyes. Like lemmings, they followed her to a waiting hearse.

"I'm not riding in that," David moaned.

"Well then you can walk. It's three blocks up the road," she smirked, gunning the engine as soon as Maggie and Stephanie were safely inside.

"Burt told us your car is in his shop," Nanette chatted. "Toby picked you guys up on the Interstate. Nice guy my brother-in-law. Lonely though. His wife drowned a couple of years back. She was having an affair with some big city dude. Toby found out. Guess she tried to drown her problems." Nanette laughed at her own joke. "They're great guys, the Raye boys. Really stick together. All our kids play together on the hockey team. The guys coach. Boys will be boys, you know. Close-knit family. Here we are. Come on inside, while I make a couple of phone calls."

"Thank you, God. Thank you, there is no wake in progress. Thank you!" Maggie prayed out loud as they walked into the empty funeral parlor.

"Wait right in here," Nanette said as she ushered them into a large living room for the dead. All the chairs faced a blank wall. Maggie and Stephanie quickly sat down and tried to absorb themselves in their own reading material. David walked in, ten minutes later, numb with cold. He began pacing and exploring, feigning indifference, picking up anything he could read.

"Who is this little prince with sunshine beaming from his finger tips?" he asked Stephanie, showing her a handful of holy picture cards.

"That's the Infant of Prague, David. There's probably a prayer on the back for someone who's died. Here, turn it over and read. Oh dear. This is for the young man in that newspaper article. He was only twenty-five. My mother used to tell me the Infant of Prague knew all your secret wishes. Where was he when this poor guy needed him?"

"Religious rubbish, Stephanie. Look at your sister. She's trying to figure out the new fashion look for spring, while you're remembering religious mumbo-jumbo." David laughed and looked over Maggie's shoulder into her magazine. He loved expensive designer clothing even more than she did.

Nanette came back with her husband, Thorn Raye. He lumbered in dressed in hunting clothes, thankfully not bearing the slightest resemblance to a mortician. Everyone breathed a sigh of relief. Now they could be on their way.

David approached him, trying to take command of the situation. Thorn faced him, assuming the somber stance of a funeral director.

"Seems there has been a bit of a misunderstanding folks. We really wanted to lend you a van for the weekend, but there is a slight problem. Some of my kin borrowed the van for hunting and we haven't cleaned it up yet. But, not to worry. I've made all the necessary arrangements at the local motel. Booked you all into a big room. Nanette will drive you there right now. I've also arranged for a rental car to pick you up in the morning. No need to delay your little vacation more than you folks already have," he smiled and began to help pick up all their belongings.

"Weren't you afraid of the liability of lending us your van?" David asked Thorn.

"You a big city lawyer or something? Folks in these parts look out for their friends and neighbors. Even take care of strangers. Even unfriendly ones."

"David's just exhausted," Stephanie intervened. "You people have restored my faith in God. We must have gotten stranded in heaven. I just don't know how to..."

"No," David interrupted. "We got stranded in Raye land."

"I think the lady wasn't finished talking, sir."

David shut up, snarling.

"Everyone is too Goddamn nice here," whispered Maggie. "Brilliant, too. They all see what a jerk David is. But you watch. I bet they're all in some major scheme to milk tourists of their money. Wait until you get the bill for this. You'll see! Too bad we can't leave David here. They'd teach him a thing or two about manners. We should have pushed him off the road when we had our chance. Are you the beneficiary of his insurance policy?"

"Stop talking like that, Maggie. I'm going to break it off with David as soon as we get home. He treats me like an imbecile. I've really had it."

"Maybe you can talk one of these red necks into knocking him off for you. Bet they'd do it."

"Maggie, stop being ridiculous. You read too much trash in your magazines."

Behind them, Nanette Raye smiled quietly, listening.

Stephanie turned around to see her and gave her a goodbye hug.

"We don't know how to thank you. I wish there was some way I could repay you, Nanette."

"Oh, you never know, Sweetie. There just may come a day when you can help us. That's what life is all about."

David was already sitting in the car while Maggie and Stephanie said some more good-byes.

"I hope business will be slow," Maggie laughed as she hugged Nanette.

"Something always comes up, Sweetie. That's just the way death is. And life," she added.


The overweight, bleached-blonde matron, behind the motel desk, could not comprehend why these two women were laughing after getting dropped off by the mortician's wife. They had to be the city folks that broke down on the Interstate. She shook her head and handed them the keys.

"We have a special room reserved for you." She smiled, displaying years of bad dentistry. David looked at her and winced.

Stephanie and Maggie raced to the room, leaving David, once again, to carry all the leftovers and suitcases into the dilapidated motel. The sisters opened and shared the bottle of complimentary white wine they found on the dresser. David declined. David never drank.

In the morning, as planned, the rental car stood waiting. No one was even surprised when Vickie Raye, the friendly rental agent, introduced herself. This Raye handed over the car and wished everyone a safe trip. Stephanie was overwhelmed with good feelings and love for the human race. Even Maggie, the family cynic, had to admit this was an incredible town. David vowed to check out Burt with the better business bureau and call the board of health about Raye's Pizza Parlor.

Their weekend passed uneventfully. Stephanie managed to stay relaxed and cheerful, content with her emotional resolution to leave David. She drove up the following Thursday, to get her car, needing the time alone to prepare for the inevitable confrontation.

She enjoyed driving the sporty rental car, leaving the city behind on her own, cruising back up the Interstate. She felt free. The day was sunny and carefree and, best of all, filled with no responsibilities other than picking up her car. The rolling hills were a soothing tonic, this ride an unexpected thrill. She pulled up to the rental agency and everyone treated her like returning royalty.

"Oh you're the pretty little woman Officer Toby Raye saved on the Interstate last week. Did you come up alone? Wait just a minute, and Vickie's husband, Billy Raye, will drive you to Burt's garage."

Fantastic! Stephanie had thought she would have to try and get a taxi in this tiny town. How silly of her. She began to daydream about living in a small village like this, a place where everyone knew everyone. Maybe even here. Possibly there was a single Raye somewhere in her future. How absurd! She was getting silly. As Billy Raye introduced himself and escorted her out the door, she noticed his wife Vickie talking seriously with Officer Toby Raye. Stephanie wanted to go and say hello. Her body heat rose to her face and she felt herself blushing. This may be the last time she ever saw Officer Toby Raye, but Billy held her firmly by the arm, steering her to his van. "What has gotten into me," she thought, looking back over her shoulder at the handsome officer, hoping for him to turn around. But he didn't.

"Call me coach," Billy smiled as he opened the door for her. "Coached the local hockey team and taught English here for 25 years. Retired this past June and opened the car rental agency."

Stephanie warmed to Billy immediately, feeling so comfortable, she didn't think it strange when he offered to take her on a little scenic tour of his cherished town.

"We've got some time to kill. Burt's not back yet. Should be back real soon, though. Gone hunting."

"I'd love to see more of this part of the valley. It's so lovely here."

"Yep, it is," Burt replied. "I know every one of these beautiful hills and valleys. Why don't we stop here at this little candle shop? It's a historic landmark."

Stephanie hopped out of the van anticipating a life without David, a life filled with new people and new experiences. "Joy to the World" was playing in the tiny candle shop as Stephanie meandered and bought an assortment of bayberry candles. She found Billy and told him they probably should be getting on their way. She had a long ride ahead of her, but this stop had really put her in the holiday spirit.

"This is a wonderful town," Stephanie said, bursting with exuberance and good will. "It must be a wonderful place to live, such peacefulness amidst these isolated farms." Stephanie turned around and put her packages in the back of the van. She noticed a hunting jacket and a coil of rope.

"Do you hunt, Billy? That's something I could never understand," Stephanie asked, turning around again in her seat.

"Only occasionally, when the need arises," Billy said, very quietly.

"Oh," Stephanie smiled not sure she understood his answer.

"There must be so much wildlife in these hills. I just don't understand hunting. The idea seems to spoil this serenity."

"There's animals all over," Billy muttered, "Good ones and bad ones," a strange new tone entering his voice. "This is a real great place to hunt. We look out for our own, here. Hunting keeps the wild animals in check."

"A young man was murdered while he was hunting. We read about it in the local paper last week in Raye's Pizza parlor? Did they find his murderer?" Stephanie asked, sincerely concerned.

"Oh, I suspect not. The guy was a real screw up. He got tangled up in a bad crowd of city boys. Started using drugs. Hit his Mama. Nearly broke her heart when he broke her rib."

The good feeling Stephanie had been experiencing began to fade. She was sorry she had asked the question.

"I found his body, hunting with some of my cousins. Stabbed twelve times," he continued, gazing at Stephanie.

"God! Toby was right. You have the prettiest green eyes. We shouldn't be talking about stuff that makes them look scared."

Stephanie shifted her gaze out to the desolate landscape, too embarrassed to look back at Billy Raye. All of a sudden she wanted to be home, back in her apartment, surrounded by hundreds of unknown neighbors. Why was she always so naive? Her sister, Maggie, would have never let herself be driven around by a total stranger.

They arrived at the garage in silence. Billy, unaware of her sudden unease, wished her a Merry Christmas.

"I saw all those candles you bought," he said with a smile. "May they light your way to the truth, and may the Baby Jesus bless you and make all your dreams come true," he waved as he pulled away. Stephanie shivered in the cold. She guessed he had grown up with the same religious stories.

"Hi there, Ma'am," Burt greeted. "Great timing, but you just missed Toby. Came by looking for you. Just got back from a little hunting trip."

Burt rifled through some paperwork looking for the bill.

"Took a little longer than usual. Those foreign cars require a little tinkering, but your car is better than new now."

Stephanie paid the bill. It was nowhere near what she had expected. Glad to be in her own car, she started the long ride home. Still a glorious sunny day, even though a few clouds had rolled in, she buckled up and chastised herself for this strange new nagging feeling. Everyone in this town had been splendid. She was sure the murderer of that young man was not one of these gentle townspeople. It had to be an outsider.

Pulling onto the Interstate, the smell of bayberry candles filled her car and she relaxed. Leonard Skynard was singing his rendition of "Knock, Knock, Knocking on Heaven's Door." Caught up in the music and the beautiful scenery, glad to be alive, she tapped her hand against the steering wheel and sang along with the melody. Life was spectacular. Huge, white, arrogant clouds had momentarily blocked the sun, leaving openings through which brilliant rays of sunshine poured. Stephanie was picturing the tiny Infant of Prague, much as he looked on the holy picture cards in Thorn's Funeral Home, right there behind the clouds, all-bejeweled, emitting those heavenly rays from his boyish fingertips, when she heard the siren and spotted the whirling red light in the rearview mirror.

Smiling, her heart beating with unexpected anticipation, Stephanie pulled over for Officer Toby Raye. What a dramatic goodbye. She rolled down her window and looked up at the handsome policeman.

"Ma'am," he said, not offering a smile. "Your sister has been trying to reach you. Seems there's some bad news at home. Your gentleman friend, David, I believe his name was, had a fatal car accident. The brakes of his BMW failed and he ran off the road. Hit a tree. I think you should come with me," he said, opening her door and putting his arms around her shoulders.

The clouds continued passing in front of the sun, the beams of light illuminating Officer Toby Raye's dark sunglasses. The last thing Stephanie saw in their reflection, before fainting into his grasp, was the puckish face of the Infant of Prague smiling at her with a mischievous grin, his eyes hidden by sporty dark lenses, grinning with satisfaction.

# Hitchin' A Ride

He stood lurking in the shadows and watched her with longing. He dared not move, lest she see him shivering, shrouded in the darkness of the narrow alley between the bar and the dilapidated tenement. A heavy fog blanketed the city, helping him to remain out of sight. The light from the dirty yellow street lamp bathed her in an eerie incandescence, illuminating her every move. She walked quickly, but obviously unsure of herself in this strange neighborhood. She glanced once behind her, as if sensing his gaze on the back of her legs. She pulled her coat around her tightly for more protection and walked faster, until she reached the safety of the address she had been seeking.

Once she passed through the doorway, he moved slowly into the night. He thought momentarily about following her inside, but the pain in his hip was a constant reminder of his last encounter through those doors. He would walk with this limp forever.

He could sense she was not from the city. She probably had a house in the country. His thoughts began to stray. He knew no other way of life. For as long as he could remember, he had lived amidst these boarded up buildings and garbage strewn alleyways. Hunger was his only constant companion, and his skin now hung in gaunt folds on his bony frame.

He crossed the street to maintain a better view of the entrance. He would not let her out of his sight again. He sat huddled against the hypnotizing warmth of the graffitied brick wall and waited.

Hours later, he saw her open the door to leave, and she was laughing. He was momentarily paralyzed. What if she was with someone? His breathing became heavy, and he was visibly shaking by the time he was sure she was leaving alone.

He slipped out into the dark shadows and stayed close to the buildings, following her right to the car. When she unlocked the door, he seized the moment and jumped into the seat beside her. She stared at him, unable to move. Fear and disbelief gripped her. He thought she was about to scream, but instead she smiled.

He was caught completely off guard. His dark eyes were on fire as he stared at her passionately. He was no longer in control. His breathing was coming in seizure-like movements. She turned to face him quietly and saw everything there was to see in his eyes. They would fill each other's needs.

She lifted her hand and touched his soft wet nose and he quickly rested his head on her lap. Spunky Dog had found a new home.

## Journey To The Garden Of The Waning Moon

Four o'clock on December 15th, the hour of deepening shadows, found Wanda uneasy. She would never get home in time. In half an hour, darkness would penetrate the valley, and she hadn't finished watering all her houseplants. She could never tend to them at night, preferring to nurture her wide variety of plants early in the morning. She doted on her plants, fawning over them like babies, like the babies that never blossomed in her womb. On days like today, she dreamed of a greenhouse, one special place for all her pet plants, eliminating the need to wander through all those lonely rooms. Years ago, she had sketched out preliminary plans. The greenhouse would be right off the living room, facing the morning sun. Now, her plants spread out over her entire house, on top of cabinets, on the dining room table, in front of every window, wherever the dwindling supply of light could be captured, appreciated and held tightly.

She sighed, thinking about the return of spring and the lengthening daylight hours to spend in her garden. She would finish watering her greenery early tomorrow morning. Wait for daylight. But really, how silly and ridiculous this whole idea had become. She vowed to fertilize and water as soon as she got home, even if she hated the idea. She sensed the upstairs plants knew their downstairs cousins had been tenderly fed. But watering plants without the sun? She couldn't really articulate how it made her feel. Futile, fruitless? December evenings, the moon waning with longing, were always the worst. Memories returned like old 55-millimeter movies running on a fast reel. Even if she had had children, they would be grown and probably married by now, happy and comfortable with their own lives. If there had been grandchildren, would they visit often? These ridiculous musings plagued her. Four o'clock, on December afternoons, even with a full and content life, they furiously phantomed, filling her with loneliness.

Pulling into her driveway, she smiled, spotting her black cat, Magic, busily grooming in the light of their bedroom window. Laughing to herself, she realized the silliness of her debate. She knew she would water the plants tonight. She had left every light on in the house. It might as well be daylight. Sam would be home shortly and, as always, she would be unsettled until the moment he walked through the door.

I must be losing it, she thought to herself. Most women get hot flashes by the time they're fifty, but here I sit in purgatory, blessed and cursed. No hot flashes, no uterus.

She unloaded the car and rushed inside, dropping bundles of Christmas presents by the door. Not wasting a moment, she filled the watering can, measured fertilizer and started to nourish her plants. The silence surrounded and perturbed her. Stopping, she turned on the stereo. Christmas carols spilled through the empty house. She immediately shut them off. Even "Silent Night" jangled her nerves. Tonight, she needed what she feared most, silence.

Just go with it, Wanda thought to herself. Maybe your body is trying to tell you something. Maybe you should try and listen to yourself for a change.

She proceeded watering the upstairs plants, her melancholy becoming so overwhelming she began to cry. She cried for a very long time, feeling silly and sad. She cried for George, his death in Vietnam and for their miscarried child, both buried deeply together, so long ago. She cried and tried to pray, hoping she remembered how. She cried for Sam and her inability to bear him children. She cried and laughed through tears, thinking of her Dad and his silly straw gardening hat. If only he could see the successful green thumb she had grown. He had loved his tiny backyard garden, tending his precious tomato plants, until the day he died, with the same love he lavished on his only daughter. She cried for her Mom, praying she'd live a few more years.

She finished fertilizing and clipped and pruned and cried, blessing her plants with her tears. She cried for the children she would never have, the grandchildren that would never be hers. She cried for her grandmother, a woman of hardy heritage, dead last month at one hundred and three. She cried for Magic's twin, Midnight, hit by a car last week. She cried for the puppy she had to give away as a child. She cried for the shame of having her childhood stolen by a family friend, a taboo she could not even discuss with Sam. Memories swirled around her at such an incessant pace, she gasped for air, drowning in their whirlpool. Exhausted, she slumped down on her bed and fell asleep.

In the stillness of dusk, her plants began to propagate. Her cleansing tears had nurtured them and they grew and grew, until Wanda lay asleep in a magnificent, verdant garden of her own making, her cat, Magic, the only witness to the growing woods.

Wanda dreamed of all the women who had preceded her, of all the women who would follow, until they became one. Humanity danced in the garden, as it grew lush and scented around her. She witnessed struggle, pain and growth. When she beheld joy, she opened her eyes. Shaking her head and rubbing her eyes, she tried to dispel the dream from her consciousness. Blinking, opening her eyes again, she timidly stood up, surveying the forest encircling her. Tentatively she took a step. She touched the trunk of the tree under which she had slept. It felt real. Where was she? What had happened? Am I dead or have I just been born?

She looked up to see the fruitful pomegranate tree under whose branches she had awakened. She remembered tasting the fruit from this tree once, possibly lifetimes ago. It had given her courage then. She reached and plucked a plump crimson snack. Savoring the tart sweet beads, she ate and was nourished. Growing more comfortable in these strange surroundings, she decided to explore.

She followed old steps down to a river and meandered along its banks, unaware the river was born from her tears. She shed her clothes and bathed. Renewed, she continued strolling, looking for the river's source. She stopped beside a clear spring that formed a lovely reflective pool. She knelt down beside the pond, gazing at her image. Plain and simple, but beautiful. She touched the tranquil water, watching her image change. She swirled the water with her fingers, faster and faster, churning the surface, finally stopping, enchanted when the water returned naturally to calm, her image intact.

Wanda wandered through meadows of daises and valleys of roses. Charity, disguised as the North Star, guided her across mountains of memories and caverns of darkness. She rested in fields of sunflowers surrounded by willows and on prairies, hugged by windswept grasses. Snow fell silently, inviting Wisdom, who drifted down on the scent of pines. Passion bounded back into the garden upon a lightning bolt, banishing forever her enemy, Fear, who wailed with the thunder of exile. Wanda took possession of her garden, the key handed to her by Hope, draped in the revealing folds of Faith, who pointed the way to the sea.

Lying in the sand, Wanda let the waves endlessly soothe her body, the constant flow washing away time. When she rose, she could view her entire garden and named it Love. Walking into the sea, slowly at first, and then with more courage, she dove down, ready to explore unknown depths. An ancient tortoise beckoned her to continue journeying on its back. Upon the tortoise's shell she traveled. The old creature revealed the mysteries of the sea and showed Wanda how to unravel the secret of time. She showed her a thousand suns and a million moons. Under the light of the waning moons, Wanda swelled, pregnant with peace, as the tortoise brought her back to shore. The Sea Goddess smiled and waddled slowly back to the sea.

Exuberant but tired (traveling always had that effect on her), Wanda recognized the pomegranate tree and decided to have another quick bite. Soon she was fast asleep.

She felt a gentle shaking of her shoulders.

"Sleeping beauty, wake up. Prince Charming is home," Sam whispered as he kissed her forehead.

"You must have been exhausted when you got home. You left all the packages in front of the door. I had to clear a path to find you. Do you feel all right? There's so much flu going around, I hope you didn't pick up a bug."

"Oh no, Sam. I feel great, rather refreshed. But, but...God, I had the strangest dream." Wanda sat up, looking all around.

Sam took Wanda's hands in his.

"Honey you look positively radiant, except your hands are freezing. Look at them. They're all clammy and puckered. They feel wet. Were you watering the plants, or have you just gotten out of the hot tub?"

"Swimming, Sam. I think I was swimming." A salty taste delighted her tongue.

"This is so bizarre. I'd better get up and move. What time is it, anyway? It gets dark so early this time of year. I can hardly tell. Let's go out for dinner. I'm starved." Wanda stood up and stretched.

"Sweetie, didn't you check the tape? I called and left a message saying I wouldn't be home for dinner. I had to go over those briefs one more time. It's 11:45, almost midnight. If you want, I'll make you an omelet."

Wanda half-smiled, a quizzical expression on her face. She tousled Sam's head of curly gray hair.

"An omelet would be wonderful. I must have been tired. I've slept for hours. Sam, I have to tell you about my dream."

Sam was not paying attention. He had pulled his handkerchief out of his jacket pocket and was wiping her lips.

"What have you been eating? You look like a little girl who's been drinking berry juice. There's a red stain all around your lips."

Wanda ran to the bathroom mirror and looked. She licked her lips, tasting the sweet tartness of pomegranate. Sam, already in the kitchen cooking one of his famous omelets, had turned on the stereo and was humming "Silent Night." Wanda walked over to him and put her arms around his waist.

"Sam, I've had a sort of unreal encounter or vision or something."

"Well you're going to have a real vision." Sam swirled her around, plopping her on a seat in the breakfast nook.

"Close your eyes, Sweetie. Merry Christmas."

When Wanda opened her eyes, formal plans for a greenhouse were spread out on the table. The attached card read:

> *To Wanda,*
> *For your magic garden*
> *Love, Sam*

Wanda buried Sam with kisses.

"Sweetie, what's that yummy taste? You have been eating berries."

"Pomegranates, Sam. I've eaten pomegranates and I can't wait to tell you where."

## Soul Proprietorship

It was only a silly piece of plastic, you know, the kind that comes in a brightly colored plastic egg. You stretch and manipulate it, then watch it ooze right back into its original form. You can even copy things from newspapers: flatten it out, press it down, and by rubbery copyright, you have an image of today's news in your hands, until you stretch it beyond capacity and the image fractures into many little pieces of goop, eventually finding its way back into one gooey malleable piece.

That's how Diedra felt today, flattened, as she played with her child's Silly Putty. Mindlessly, she stretched it and plastered it against the newsprint of today's paper, a paper she hadn't even bothered to read. Exhausted, as usual, she had just lost another and maybe final battle with her husband. They seemed to argue over everything, yet nothing, these days. She asked him for one day. One lousy day! She didn't want to drive to Vermont in this blizzard by herself and she couldn't leave here until she knew the results of her mother's latest biopsy. Diedra wasn't sure if she would make the trip at all, yet he couldn't wait one lousy day for her in case she really needed to get away.

Diedra's mother was handling her own cancer with a miraculous calm. Diedra was terrified of her mother's illness. While her mom lived every day with robust vitality, waiting to die, Diedra felt as if she were dying a little every day, waiting to live. Her spirit was missing lately, and it wasn't just since her mom had gotten sick. Her husband, Bennett, worked later and later each evening. His career was skyrocketing and an aura of success surrounded him. The higher he soared, the lower Diedra felt. Her career was put on hold until the kids were a little older, but her thoughts always scattered, wandering to the many places she had dreamed of visiting as a photo-journalist. That career never materialized, but Diedra still loved to write and take photographs. Professional quality photos of their children filled every inch of wall space but writing took time and she could never find any.

Diedra, the stay-at-home mom, didn't have a *real* job, so it was Diedra who took her mom to all the chemo sessions; it was Diedra everyone called to pick up dogs at the kennel, run bake sales, and generally be everyone's best buddy. Maybe that was why she felt so completely let down today when Bennett refused to postpone, by even a day, leaving for their ski condo. She wanted someone in her corner for a change, worrying about her.

"I'm really losing it," she thought as the oven timer went off. She squished the silly piece of plastic back into a ball and got up to take the apple pie out of the oven to cool. The house smelled all homey and loved with the scent of cinnamon and nutmeg hanging in the air. Bennett would want to take the pie to Vermont. Bennett's sister, Shaari, her husband Wayne, and their kids were already there. Even Diedra and Bennett's twin girls, Olivia and Brenda, were already up in Vermont with their cousins. Sammy wanted to stay and drive up with his Daddy.

Diedra plodded upstairs and sat down at her computer. She felt blank. The novel she had been working on for two years didn't sound right. The voice wasn't hers. It sounded phony, stale, dead; it sounded exactly as she felt. Starting to pound the keys with a vengeance, she remembered the silly piece of goop she had left on the kitchen table. If Barney, their mixed breed mutt, got it off the table, there would be a mess. Sammy would scream when he got home from kindergarten wondering where it had gone. Gone? It would be all over the dog and their new rug. Bennett would blame her, as usual, for not paying attention to anything. She trudged back down to the kitchen, picked up the egg, and tossed it into her pocket, petting Barney on the top of his big, ever-hungry head. "He probably would have eaten it," she mused, climbing back up the stairs.

Staring at the computer screen, she rolled the egg in her hands, waiting for thoughts to come and direct the blank page. She slipped out the oozy plastic and started to play with it. She flattened it on the printed page of her first draft and lifted the print. She did it again and again until thousands of black letters blurred into oblivion on the plastic putty. She stretched it, watching the print disappear into a nondescript blur. She tried to focus on this blur to detect just when the words became indecipherable; just when did her marriage become only bearable?

She slapped the slime down again, but this time on a glossy page in a book on dried flowers. 'It will never pick up this print,' she thought to herself, but it did, colors and all. She stretched the goop and stretched it, until she lost herself in the field of red and brilliant poppies, swaying in the sun. She was a little girl again; Daddy was lifting her high on his shoulders. She could feel the warm sun on her hair. Daddy slid her down off his shoulders and gave her a little plastic egg, like the one she had bought Sammy. They sat down on the cool green grass and played with it in the meadow beside her old school. She felt the relaxation of youth spread through her body. Squishing the plastic over a hard rock, she lifted it to see the fine indentations of centuries of wear telling its own tale.

Just as suddenly, she was sitting on a huge boulder. Kids were taunting her, calling her weird; her poem had won first prize in the school magazine contest. She ignored their taunts. The rock, this meadow, were all her friends. She felt grounded and in touch with life out here, more than in any classroom.

She took the silly plastic out of her coat pocket and stretched it over her poem, covering it from invading eyes, and then bounced the plastic down the hill. She watched it bounce into the future where it landed on the football field years later. She was leading the band as drum majorette. She never thought she would pass the tryouts, grueling weeks of practicing and coordination, but she was determined and succeeded. Her high school band won the competition that season, and Bennett, her high school sweetheart, won her heart at the local pizza hangout by the river. He carved their names inside a heart, in ink, on the wooden table and pressed the silly plastic over it to make an impression. He did. She lost her virginity that night and a small piece of her soul. Several weeks later she realized she was pregnant. It was years before she ever wrote again or felt she could accomplish anything on her own. Oh, she published a poem here and there, and a story or two, but could never quite find the time to finish her novel. It wasn't that she didn't love her life, it just revolved around everyone else.

'Where does a soul go when it is lost?' she wondered. Daydreaming and still rolling the plastic between her fingers, she plastered it down on her own mouse pad, that empty void of gray. Picking it up, expecting to see the tiny granule impressions of the plastic square, her eyes squinted in disbelief, as she read "Bennett & Dee-Dee Forever," surrounded by a heart. Fearing for her sanity, she squished the plastic into a ball once more and tried it again. This time, she carefully lifted the plastic goop off the mouse pad. The image she saw shocked her. Proudly posing for the local newspapers, she stood with the high school band's trophy held high over her head. Diedra sighed, no longer in awe of the plastic toy. Back then, she thought she could accomplish anything. She was just dreaming. More amused than frightened now, actually more certain she was having a breakdown, she applied the plastic, one more time, to the mouse pad. Curiously, she lifted it. The poppies in the meadow of her youth filled the room with their strong musky scent. They were red, vibrant and luxurious, demanding she get some fresh air. Spring was around the corner, even though blanketed by white.

She listened to the poppies and went to get her coat, taking the Silly Putty, in its egg, with her. She bundled up with snow boots, a hat and gloves. Barney loved the snow so she decided to take him along. Time to take a long walk before she really lost 'it'. On second thought, finding 'it', whatever it might be, was an intriguing possibility.

She grabbed a scarf and knotted it around her neck to keep out the awakening wind. She walked for over two hours. She lifted her feet, listening to the crunch in the white silence. Her heart recaptured the hidden sun. Finally, exhausted, she found a rock, sat down and let memories flood over her. She took the silly egg out of her coat pocket and opened it. Brushing the rapidly accumulating snow off the rock, Diedra pressed the inanimate goop against the hard surface. She smiled at a passing cross-country skier enjoying the day in the park. When she lifted the plastic, an impression of every tiny little defect and perfection of the rock's surface was displayed in an intricate pattern. Diedra smiled and began to laugh, a long, loud, hearty laugh she hadn't enjoyed in ages. "Well I'll be darned," she said to the rock. "I know where to look for your soul when it's gone." There was no one there to hear her discovery. The skier had swiftly moved on. She smoothed the plastic goop over the palm of her hand. Seriously lifting it off, she studied the tiny lines running across her palm to all five fingers. Their mirror image was imprinted in the goop. "I know who you are," she smiled to the plastic as she tucked it back into its shell.

She walked home with a spring in her step, a spring missing for a long time, and laughter in her eyes, every passerby acknowledged. Bennett was just pulling into the driveway when she came home.

"Hon, what are you doing out in this weather? It's getting dark."

"Just taking a walk. Sammy is at a friend's house, but he should be home any moment. He's all packed and ready to go. The twins left with your sister this morning. I hope you have a wonderful time, Darling."

"Hon, I feel awful about leaving you. I really do. This has been hard on me as well. I just really need to get away."

"I know you do. It's OK. I've decided I'm not going up. Mom has the most wonderful attitude in the world. I want to be there with her. Do you know what she said to me when they were wheeling her down for this biopsy? Be brave, she told me! Me! I should be brave. She's the one who's had three cancer surgeries in three years and I should be brave. I'd forgotten I come from such strong stuff."

"Well, I'll spend the weekend skiing with the gang and come home late Sunday night. I'll miss you sweetheart. Thanks for being so understanding. Are you sure you're OK?"

"Yes, I'm OK. Thanks for forcing me to be, Bennett," she whispered into his ear and tenderly kissed him on the cheek. "I found this today. It's been missing for some time."

"Sammy will be delighted; it's that silly little plastic goop that he loves so much. Here give it to me so he'll have it in Vermont. I'll throw it right in my pocket."

Bennett took the little plastic egg and placed it in his jacket pocket. Diedra gently fished it out again. "I think I'll buy Sammy another one. I kind of messed this one up with ink. It has my imprint on it."

"Hmm, Dee-Dee," he said, calling her by the name he used when they were just kids, "the fresh air really becomes you. You should walk more often. You look like you're fourteen again."

"I don't feel like fourteen, Bennett; suddenly I feel very grown up. Come on, let's go in the house."

They went inside and she watched Bennett pack. Sammy came home anxious to be going and Diedra sent them off with hugs and kisses. That empty feeling was gone. She sat down to write. The words flowed, slowly at first, and then with the same rhythm she loved and trusted.

Hours later, she stretched and rested her eyes. The plastic egg was lying right there alongside her computer where she had tenderly placed her new prized possession. She had promised, with her heart and soul, to buy Sammy a new one. She pulled out the Silly Putty.

"I really know who you are," she said to the slimy plastic goop in the egg. "And, I'll never lose you again." She leaned back and smiled, finished with chapter ten, content at last, understanding the meaning of true soul proprietorship.

# Cookie

**C**an you ask the owners for this recipe? These happen to be the most delicious peanut butter cookies I've ever tasted. Let me take a few more for the road." Ted mumbled these words with his mouth full of the sweets, grabbing another handful of cookies from the Lenox china plate on the spotless kitchen counter.

Buffy shifted her weight uneasily, from one stylish Ferragamo pump to the other, staring at the decreasing pile of cookies and the crumbs all over the counter.

"I tell the owners to bake homemade cookies for the ambiance. You know, you're in advertising, like a staging effect, so the house will smell all comfy and homey. I don't think they expected to find half the plate of cookies eaten," Buffy tried to say in as light-hearted a tone as she could muster. Never annoy the client, she kept telling herself, with a pinched smile on her lips.

"Now, now, Miss Buffy Gibbons, I think your hair band is on a little too tight. You do want to make a sale today, don't you? I'd really like to get this over and done with this weekend. Of course, I can buy the *For Sale by Owner Magazine* and go about this on my own," Ted muttered with the last remnant of a peanut butter cookie in his mouth.

Crumbling his sixth napkin, for as many cookies, he wiped his lips and mustache and smiled. "This house isn't really my style anyway. Too comfy and homey. Get my drift? But do get me that recipe."

Buffy Gibbons, really Penelope Krushnicki Gibbons, before she moved to Darien, Connecticut, scooped up the soiled napkins and the list of houses she intended to show Ted today. He was the best referral she'd had in months, maybe years. Thank heavens that realtor in New Jersey had remembered her. She had met Monica Osborn briefly at the last real estate convention in Hartford. They had shared a sumptuous lunch at the croissant sandwich counter where they both indulged their hunger, licking Brie off their fingers in satisfaction, ignoring the fruit and yogurt bar at the convention site where most of the other svelte real estate matrons nibbled on grapes. In her brief referral letter, Monica, the realtor from New Jersey, stated she could not find anything there to fill Ted's appetite for a home of his own. Ted, a wealthy, confirmed bachelor and Manhattanite, said he owned his own advertising agency. Monica thought maybe Buffy could find something to satisfy Ted's tastes in Connecticut. And here he was. One house down and the day just beginning.

"Anyway, I can't believe they call this a contemporary. It's really an overpriced raised ranch," Buffy remarked, trying to sound very off-handed while carefully rewrapping the plate of cookies, sweeping any telltale crumbs into the palm of her hand and depositing them dutifully into the trash.

"Let's go now, Dear. No more cookies," she scolded like the stalwart matron she was on her way to becoming. Buffy glanced in the hall mirror to fluff up her bangs and smooth her neat, chin-length pageboy. She looked back over her shoulder to see Ted snatching one more cookie.

"Dear? Aren't we getting intimate rather quickly," he chuckled, covering the dish and neatly depositing the napkin in the trash. "See what a good boy I am."

Buffy looked into his mischievous green eyes. With his white hair and beard, he really was very attractive. Maybe something more could come of this. She hated this job, but it was the only thing she could think of to do when Brad, her husband of twenty years, left her for his dingbat young secretary. She thought she would love being a real estate agent, but she really loved her old life style, tennis games, golf, and dinner at the club and best of all not having to work for any of it.

"It's not a term of endearment," she smiled, "but it could be."

She immediately felt stupid and ill. That dumb remark could cost her a sale. What if he had a girlfriend or was engaged or even gay? All the sincere ones were gay anyway today.

"Get me that cookie recipe and you never know," he smiled back, placing his hand gently on her shoulder as they exited the house and walked to her seven year old hunter green Jeep Cherokee.

"The next home we will be seeing is a contemporary colonial. The owners are very anxious to sell. They have already been transferred to California. It's only three blocks away. Wait until you see all the dogwood trees along the street. It's a perfect time to show this house; they're all in bloom. We'll be there momentarily."

Ted had been sitting beside Buffy in the passenger seat, observing her nervous twitter and her St. John Knit suit.

"Do you have a real name?" he suddenly asked as they pulled into the driveway of a rambling discombobulation of a house.

"That is my real name," Penelope snapped. "Well at least that's what everyone calls me," she softened, not wanting to lose a sale.

"Well, I don't want to call you Buffy. What is your real name?"

Buffy sat with her hand on the ignition key staring at the house ahead.

"Penelope," she hissed between clenched teeth. "It's really Penelope."

"OK, Penelope, let's see what a contemporary colonial looks like. A contradiction of terms, if you ask me, but I'm here to buy a house, so let's go in and see."

Penelope got out of the car, negotiating the muddy driveway, carefully placing her stylish, but sensible, mid-height heels carefully on the few tiny patches of dry gravel.

"Seems they have a bit of a drainage problem here, don't they?" Ted remarked, running around to offer his arm as they precariously avoided the large puddles.

"Oh, a building inspector would have to take a look at this."

"You don't need a building inspector to call this one."

Penelope fumbled with the lock box while looking up at the sky. Rain was imminent. She hoped these owners had fixed the dining room leak before leaving for California.

"Hmm, now what's that I smell?" Ted queried, bee-lining into the kitchen. "I thought these folks already moved to California."

Making himself right at home in the kitchen, Ted was devouring the chocolate chip cookies Penelope had baked there earlier this morning.

Smiling with annoyance and some amusement now, she chided, "Boy you are a hungry Jack."

"Ted, Ted is the name, Lassie, and yes I love a good cookie. How did these get here?"

"Lassie is a dog, a boy dog, besides. And I made those cookies," she beamed boastfully. "That's the one thing I was good at in my marriage, making stupid cookies," she mumbled under her breath, her mood changing quickly.

Ted, seemingly not listening, was polishing off one cookie after another. He opened the refrigerator and helped himself to a glass of ice-cold milk.

"Are you done?" Penelope asked, hands on her hips like an old school marm. "Now I have to clean this up."

"These folks aren't in California yet are they? All their furniture is still here."

"We told them to leave the furniture. The house shows better. They're living in a hotel until their God damn house sells." Penny flushed, embarrassed by her sudden outburst.

A loud boom of thunder echoed through the house.

"See! Shouldn't take the Lord's name in vain, Penelope. God gets angry when you do."

"By the way, what was your last name? You know. Who did you grow up as Penelope? Here, try one of your cookies. How come the house still smells so good?"

"Because I made them *here* this morning, you fool. The owners really are in California." I have got to get this situation under control, she fumed to herself.

"How industrious. Have one anyway. You're a good cook, Penny, but actually this house isn't for me. I really was thinking of waterfront."

Penny whirled around from the sink, quickly putting the glass back in the cabinet.

"Brightened up your day, didn't I? I can afford it. Don't speculate. What have you got to show me?"

"Well, let's see," Penny answered, trying to conceal her excitement. "I've got to make a phone call first."

Penelope whipped her cell phone out of her Nantucket Pocket Book, about the only thing it could hold, and walked into the dining room to make the appointment. She looked up. Rainwater was beginning to drip from the ceiling. Her heart raced. The commission on 4.5 million would be what? Thank God. No answer. The owners couldn't delay this showing. She would use the lock box. She heard the cabinets opening and went in to see Ted happily munching handfuls of chips from a previously unopened bag and washing them down with a beer.

"What are you doing? This is not your home. Let's go," Penny rushed, ignoring the empty beer can he threw in the sink and failing to close or put away the open bag of potato chips.

"We are just so lucky to see this next house. No one is there now so we can take our time looking around," Penny babbled, locking the door behind this last listing. "The damn roof leaks here anyway," she offered, even though Ted had not seen the constant drip that had begun to trickle from the dining room ceiling.

"Oh no, it's pouring."

"Only water, Penny. Let's make a run for it."

Penny could feel her suit shrinking, her shoes squishing and her hair curling as she ran for the car. This was humiliating. She turned on the ignition and looked into the mirror trying to smooth her pageboy.

"Let it be, Penny. God, your hair is curly. It's turning up in all these little cute spirals."

"*Aahhh!*" Penny politely screamed. "It takes me hours to blow-dry it straight."

"And just as many hours once a month to color it blonde, I suspect," Ted observed.

Penny blushed right up to her dark roots. Her hair band had slipped, exposing her secret. She would never make this sale and Ted was starting to annoy her. Trying to maintain some decorum, she chose to ignore his last remark and backed out a little too swiftly from the narrow, muddy driveway, nicking her front fender on the crumbling retaining wall.

"Easy now, Sugar Dumpling. That will take a bite out of your commission."

Penny looked at him with exasperation. "You will love this next house. I promise," she prayed.

Penny beamed as they pulled into the next long driveway. Willow trees lined the long drive, culminating in a picturesque view of Long Island Sound.

"Well, now we're on to something," Ted excitedly exclaimed, leaping out of the car before Penny could even come to a complete halt.

Penny searched for her umbrella. The rain was coming down hard now and Ted was already at the front door, looking slightly disheveled but all the more gorgeous. Her umbrella nowhere in sight, Penny decided, to hell with it, and made a dash for the doorway. She was positively soaked by the time she opened the lock box. Breathtaking views greeted them. Even Penny was startled by the gray blustery landscape before their eyes, the view even more magnificent in the storm.

"Well, well, well my precious Penny. What an exquisite place to sit and have lunch."

"Lunch?" Penny almost shouted. "We haven't even seen the house yet and you want to send out for lunch."

"No, not send out for lunch. Let's see what's in the fridge." Ted opened the refrigerator as if he already owned the house. He removed two large heads of Romaine lettuce, a jar of anchovies, and a lemon. "Let's see," he mumbled to himself, "they must have black olives and olive oil around here somewhere." He proceeded to open every cabinet until he found the needed ingredients.

"Nice. Extremely well stocked cabinets. How does a fresh Caesar Salad sound or would you prefer something warm? God, you look beautiful wet. Your hair is full of ringlets." Ted removed her hair band and tousled her unkempt wet curls. "I think you should dye your hair back to its original color, chestnut, I would guess."

"You can't just make yourself at home here. We'll get sued or arrested or something."

"Now, now, pretty Penny, learn to live a little," he smiled while decorking an expensive bottle of merlot from the wine rack. "A little lunch will do you good. Is red OK? We have to let it breathe."

Knocked out of her sense of normalcy, Penny didn't know how to respond and stared at him dumbly.

"Here, take off those shoes and dry off a bit. Actually why don't you get out of those wet clothes? I'll be right back." Ted left on his own to find the master bedroom and came back with a pink terrycloth robe. "Here, go in there and put this on. I like this house. It could work."

Shocked, but thinking of the glorious commission on this huge sale, she moved her body into trance-like action. She emerged from the bathroom barefoot and clothed in pink terrycloth. Ted had the table set, wine poured and a fire going in the fireplace.

"Cozy, isn't it?" he smiled, again. "You will feel better after you eat."

Penny sat down opposite Ted and tried to smile. She was suddenly ravenous. Ted had already eaten his first helping of salad and a half a loaf of warm French bread he must have found somewhere and heated up. He was opening a second bottle of wine as Penny finally devoured her salad.

"You never told me what your last name was."

Penny blushed. "Krushnicki. Kind of like the Polish Cookie."

"Why, Cookie, that's what I'll call you. Cookie. I knew Buffy Gibbons was not your real name. Cookie, tell me something. Do you like dessert?"

"No, no. We have to get out of here."

"I make the meanest soufflé."

"Here, look what I found in the upstairs bathroom," he said producing the drugstore box like a priceless jewel. "The owner must color her hair. All natural chestnut hair color. Guaranteed to condition and shine. Now go upstairs and put this little magic to work and I'll take care of the kitchen and dessert."

Already lost, and whirling from the wine, Cookie did as she as told, not sure if the thought of a huge commission was driving her on or temporary insanity.

A half hour later, the white fluffy towels of the master bedroom and the pink robe all stained with hair dye, Cookie assessed her new look in the mirror. Her cheeks were glowing and so was her hair, which resembled a mild Afro. Is this what she really looked like? Kicking the towels and the robe out of the way, she opened the owner's closet and surveyed the contents. She chose a pair of black leather pants, a low cut black sweater and five-inch-high black heels. How fortunate the owner was her exact size.

A little wobbly at first, either from the wine or the heels, Cookie began her descent down the stairs. The aroma of caramelized sugar filled her nostrils. Ted was waiting at the table ready to serve dessert.

"Made a mousse instead. Had to use the ingredients at hand. Wow, don't you look spectacular. Here sit, sit down," he ordered, pulling the chair out for her.

"Why would you ever want to be blonde?"

"I'm not sure what I did to my hair, or my life," Cookie giggled, digging into the tasty mousse. "You are one hell of a good cook."

"Most misfits are," he winked, polishing off his second dessert. "Do you like to dance?"

"Why, yes, although I haven't in quite some time."

"Looks like a good stereo system they have here. Let's see what's in their CD collection, Cookie. Look here, Tina Turner, *Private Dancer*. Dance for me, Cookie."

"What?"

"Dance for me."

Ted put on the music.

Feeling totally outside of herself, Cookie got up and ever so slowly put her arms around Ted's neck. She began swaying to the rhythm. The fire crackled and the wine flowed. Ted kissed the nape of her neck, pulling the sweater off one shoulder.

"I'm really not myself right now," Cookie whimpered.

"I'm not who you think I am either," he whispered back.

"Neither am I, any more," Cookie sighed back.

Mesmerized by the ridiculousness of this strange day, Cookie twirled in Ted's arms, her head spinning with vertigo and wine. She felt as if she could sell every house in Darien. In one final twirl, Ted grabbed her around the waist and held her tight as he dipped her backward. It was in this lovely, abandoned, reckless tangoed position, that she saw the front door open, and the Morgans walk in. As Ted lifted her slowly, her gaze went from their knees, to their astonished faces, to Ted's winning smile. With his arm around her waist to steady her, he walked them both to face the startled homeowners, smiling his award-winning grin.

"Pete and Sally Morgan, I'd like you to meet Cookie. She just sold me your house."

# Sunflower

Ariel started life in a little, black, hard shell with a tiny white stripe down the middle. She was comfortably surrounded by many others just like herself. Life was reassuring and perfectly planned. One day, as expected, she was mechanically plucked and neatly packaged with all the others and shipped far away from home. She was dumped into a clear plastic environment where one by one she watched those around her being gobbled up by the scary world around them. Ariel was frightened. She had these tremendous yearnings as if she were about to split at the seams with a powerful energy. She knew there had to be more to her life than simply being eaten up by the world. One by one her friends disappeared until she was the only one left. She was then rather harshly flung outside and into the grass. A huge, handsome, dark bird saw her and immediately swooped down and swallowed her whole. Not knowing any better, she believed she was in love. She lived within the confines of his being until he expelled her somewhere out over the vast ocean. Ariel, now rather saturated and plump, was terrified and unprepared. She felt herself settle into the sandy bottom and feel sort of safe. Life became comfortable and predictable, if rather soggy, but soon those old stirrings began. She started to flirt with a fish and he too devoured her with gusto. She knew it wouldn't last. They were just not the same but Ariel was bored and ready for adventure and it was a good thing. Ariel's once beloved fish was caught by a clever fisherman and became his dinner. Ariel felt positively fried when she woke up and discovered she was surrounded by a heap of fish bones on a sunny hilltop. She settled down into a dirty little hole she called her own and as exhausted and dead as she felt, something old and familiar began to stir within her. She knew she could just burst. She would not be contained. She reached for the sun and began growing in leaps and bounds. She followed her heart and felt she could reach the clouds. Encouraged now by others like her, she continued to grow until she was gloriously crowned with a yellow halo of petals, the fulfillment of her own being. She gave birth to many little black seeds that resembled her old self, but she wasn't hard and brittle anymore. She knew what she was, a sunflower. For many years to come, she would tell other little nutty seeds that no seed is ever too old to sprout. Sometimes it just has to be eaten, and buried and expelled and rained upon by life if it is ever to bloom.

Dianalee Velie

## The Baby Born In 1944

> After the paintings: *The Baby (1944)*
> and *Artist's Daughter by the Sea (1943)*
> by Milton Avery

Why I was thrown into the world at a time of such violence and destruction, I will never know. But birth always comes through death. Try as they might, adults seem to forget this. It is only we, nameless, faceless, infants who still hold the memories of the past and the future. We, who still know that we come tumbling into the future on a bright blue carpet of hope, plummeting out of the straight-backed history of our parents into a new rounder, more encompassing view of the world. Every generation is the same, but coming into the world in 1944 made the memories of the recent past hard to comprehend. Why had I returned? I know it was my choice. I looked at the pale pink bunting my mother had dressed me in. There was nothing else to look at. Mother was in the other room crying. She had not heard from my father. I knew he would be dead in a few weeks. I had already heard talk of his arrival before I left for earth. I tried to put myself into my mother's emotions. I was once again remembering time. I thought forward to the day I would wear a dress of almost that same color pink. With matching pink socks, I would be the picture of youthful innocence at the seashore, collecting conch shells while listening to waves echoing the pulls and tugs in my body. The gulls would hover around me that day, trying to protect my innocence, but I knew it was over. I knew by the way he wanted to take my photo that he was looking for so much more. Strategically he placed the shells between my legs and my hand between my bent up knees. The world was on the verge of another war and I was on the verge of losing my virginity. This war would not pull the nation together. This one would tear at its very soul. Here I would come of age. We nameless, faceless babes, born way back then in 1944, knew this would all come to pass. Knew we would lose our innocence before we were ready. Knew we were a generation that would turn against each other, but yet, ... knowing all we did at birth, we still chose to ride a magic blue carpet of hope with the eternal wish that with each birth, the bright blue blanket would grow.

# The Seed

*She wanted her child to feel no pain*
*to be happy and carefree,*
*to never feel the sorrow*
*of unrequited love*
*or the anguish*
*of dreams unfulfilled,*
*to walk only in sunlight*
*while listening*
*to the music of the eternal spheres.*
*She wanted to give birth to a dream.*

excerpt from *The Messiah Among Us*
by Tamar Davidson

After filling the bird feeder to capacity, Tammy scattered the remaining seed on the frozen ground. Her dark auburn curls captured flyaway seeds, which she shook out of her hair with the rapidly falling snowflakes. Several of these errant seeds, having fallen inside her boots, pinched at her feet. 'Maybe if I just stand here in the storm,' she thought, giggling, 'the cardinals will come and feast right off of me.' The snow whirled faster as Tammy stuck her tongue out to catch some dancing flakes. 'In two minutes I'll look like a pregnant snow woman. I do hope the cardinals come back.' Mesmerized by the visiting cardinals these last few days, Tammy had made it an everyday practice to keep the feeder full. Against today's snow, the birds would glimmer like rubies.

Tammy clomped up the back stairs, hands resting on her aching back, almost slipping. Carefully now, she held onto the railing. She must be more careful. In her seventh month of pregnancy, she felt clumsy and awkward. This constant back pain was something new. Stomping the snow off her boots, she opened the sliding glass door to her newly remodeled kitchen. She was shocked to find her father-in-law, Judd, in her not so Kosher home, eating a sandwich made with rye bread and pork kielbasa. Tammy had bought the sausage yesterday at the Polish butcher in her home town, to satisfy her craving for the tastes of her childhood. Judd probably thought no one was home when he decided to satisfy himself with this forbidden meal.

"Hi," Tammy called, brushing the snow off her jacket as she walked into the kitchen. Judd wiped his mouth with a paper towel, finishing his meal without guilt. As she watched him, nausea churned her stomach. She wanted so badly to love this distant man.

"Oh," he smiled ruefully. "What are you doing home? Did you get that sausage from the new Kosher butcher in town? It's pretty good, hey." He winked knowingly at her.

Hardly believing her ears, she felt faint and had to sit down. What was *she* doing here? This was her home. What was *he* doing here unannounced and uninvited? Here was the man who had made her life hell when he had disowned his only son, Seth, for falling in love with her, Tammy the *shiksa*. Now he was pretending he didn't know he had just polished off a Polish pig sandwich. For years, all those years, Judd had made her feel like the swine he had just devoured. Judd and his wife Shully had only accepted her as their daughter-in-law after she converted to Judaism. She made this concession, after constant pressure from Seth; Seth, who once declared he was agnostic. "All religion is a farce," were the words she recalled, but that was then and this was now.

She had been driven by her own needs then. Raised by parents whose devoted love for their only child caused them to be over protective, she craved new experiences when she went away to college. Seth was a new experience, Judaism another.

She memorized the Hebrew prayers for her conversion; how foreign and strange they sounded on her tongue. She truly loved the best of both religions, the Catholicism in which she was raised and now the ancient laws of Judaism. Seth was furious, though, when she referred to her conversion as her second baptism. Tammy dreamt she would be a bridge of love and understanding between the two faiths. She soon realized that illusion was impossible to accomplish. Daily, Seth's religion grew in stature for him, somehow usurping his love for Tammy. Why did she ever think she could change centuries of mistrust and hate?

And now, with the imminent birth of their first child, Seth immersed himself in his religion. He resented her adamant refusal to discontinue celebrating Christmas with her family, reaffirming Tammy's belief: organized religion was unimportant and in certain cases destructive; God belonged in your heart. Tammy once wrote beautiful lyrical poetry about her relationship with God. Poetry filled with laughter and reverence. The poems came back to her from Seth, always marked up in red pen. That's how they met. Seth was her writing professor, sophomore year at Sarah Lawrence College. Repeatedly, he told her she showed no real talent.

Comments like, "Shows some knowledge of the craft, but please write about what you know! Start with simpler subjects. Not God!" filled the margins of her papers. She continued to write poetry, even after their affair and subsequent marriage, but she no longer shared the poems with Seth. She wrote intimately about what she knew, Her God, although she had never encountered The Almighty in a church or synagogue.

○

Now, she looked blankly at her father-in-law.

"You know that's pork, Dad. You saw Seth have a fit yesterday when I brought it home. I had such a craving!"

"Well now, now, young lady, you told me it was Kosher beef sausage didn't you? Isn't Seth expected home soon?"

Tammy held onto the chair arms for support. Even though her head was still wet with melting snow, she felt as if a heat wave had broken out over her body. Sweat came dripping off her eyebrows as Sunflower, her pet cat, tried to jump into her disappearing lap. Tammy lifted her pet, petting and stroking her soft fur while desperately swallowing unshed tears. She looked longingly at the cradle her Dad had made for the upcoming birth of his first grandchild. She missed her parents in Florida so much; she wanted this baby so much. Through dizziness and nausea she could barely hear what her father-in-law was saying.

"Yes, Seth said he wanted to show me the ultrasound pictures. It's a son we are going to have. You have made us all so proud. We will name him Samuel. Maybe he will be the Messiah."

"We will name *her* Kristin," Tammy managed to stammer, knowing this would put a stop to the conversation.

In the following momentary silence, Seth walked in the front door.

"Hi, Tammy, I didn't know you would be home. I told Dad to meet me here for lunch."

"He's already eaten, Seth. He ate a lovely kielbasa sandwich with kosher mustard."

"Ah, what a joke she makes," Judd snickered, never looking at Tammy.

"Tammy, that is not even funny. Things are going to change here after the baby is born, and take down that Christmas wreath on the front door."

"You used to love Christmas before we were married, Seth. Besides, it's not a Christmas wreath. It's only evergreens, a sign of hope for the holiday season. I even put a blue bow on it for Hanukkah."

"We are not going to get into an argument about this in front of my father. What are you trying to do, disgrace this family pretending my father has eaten pork? Are you trying to ruin his reputation? This pregnancy has turned you into a story teller."

"Excuse me, Seth. I am not lying. He not only polished off a whole pork sandwich, he .... Extreme nausea over took Tammy. She stumbled to the bathroom. No one followed her. Months had passed since Seth had even touched her. Lying in bed at night, she would beg for his touch, even his arms around her would have sufficed, but he would close his eyes and mumble about exhaustion and the alarm clock. He'd soon be snoring, while Tammy prayed silently in bed for a healthy daughter.

"Dear God, forgive me," she prayed now. "Let my baby be healthy, boy or girl it doesn't matter." Over and over she repeated Hail Marys to her heavenly Mother. "Please, please, do not forsake me now," she prayed as her body convulsed in spasm. Was anybody listening? What had she done? Oh God, what had she done?

Last year when the doctor told them about Seth's negative sperm count, the solution to their problem seemed so simple. Now she lay on the cold marble floor, horrified. She had no idea who was the real father of her baby. Oh, the world would think it was Seth's child, but the sperm that had fertilized her egg was made up of a concoction of Seth's brother's sperm and his father Judd's. Tammy shivered. She was probably carrying Judd's child in her womb, all those months of treatments and injections, all to have a child to love and be loved by. Convinced she is having a son, they have already named her child, Samuel. The doctor had said she wasn't sure. She had said it was just a possibility. The baby was not in a good position to really determine its sex.

Finally, there was a knock on the bathroom door.

"Tammy, I think you should come out and apologize to my father."

The words fell like ice cubes on the cold marble. Where was the brilliant professor with whom she had fallen in love?

"Tammy, come out now. I know you're not yourself these days." His tone had turned. He was treating her in the same condescending manner with which Judd spoke to his wife. Tammy wanted to stop her world, make them go away, erase the torment and the pain she had endured, erase everything but the new life in her. She remained on the bathroom floor and wept.

She heard Adam speaking with his father and thought she heard them leave the house. In the stillness she dozed. When she finally woke up, her back flamed with pain and her face was as alabaster as the snow outside. She slowly managed to creep upstairs and fall into bed. Night had blanketed the earth and Seth had not returned. Busy helping another young coed with a late term paper, Tammy barely had the energy to assume.

Seth wasn't in bed beside her when the contractions started. She should have called an ambulance, but the phone was out. She watched the big red stain spread beneath her onto to the king-size white sheets. Weakly, she reached into her bedside table drawer, clutched her hidden rosary beads and prayed.

○

Chaos reigned while the plans for the funeral were arranged. The baby was tended to in the appropriate Orthodox manner. They would not give Tammy a Jewish burial; she had, after all, died with her rosary in hand. Her inconsolable parents claimed her body, burying her in a quiet nonsectarian cemetery near their home in Florida where a palm tree bent gracefully over Tammy's grave. At Seth's insistence, they took all of Tammy's belongings from his house. Too overwhelmed with grief, they stored her personal effects in her old room and locked the door. They visited the grave site often, feeling weaker and older each time, leaning on each other more and more for support.

Years passed before time slowly began to heal their wound and they found the strength to start going through Tammy's personal papers. They were mesmerized by hundreds of pages of poetry, many of the poems containing  highly critical commentaries in the margins, written by Seth. As they read through Tammy's poems, she seemed to be right there beside them. They shared her poetry with some very close friends who lived in the same condominium complex. People began to comment, repeating lines and verses, finding comfort, truth and beauty in the inspiring words. This sharing eased their grief. The sound of Tammy's poems floated on the breezes of South Florida and soon the sound of her words circulated around the country. Posthumously, she gained a following. Her poetic insights brought truth to her admirers around the world. Reading Tammy's poetry changed people in subtle ways. Tammy lived on through her words. Many of her followers made the journey to her cemetery plot and placed flowers on her grave. Many sat there for hours and meditated.

○

More years quietly passed. Tammy's elderly parents continued to tend her grave, organizing the ever present new bouquets, taking away the old ones, and chatting with her many devotees. Unpredictable weather patterns had confused the nation this year. Weathermen were blaming El Niño for the strange weather across the globe and now it was snowing in Florida. On this particular day, a young women of about twenty-one stood beneath the palm tree looking at Tammy's headstone. She placed a spray of evergreens, tied in a blue bow, on the pure white snow covering Tammy's grave. She had just graduated from college and wanted to be a writer. The works of Tamar Davidson had always inspired her. Now she wept from the shock of truth. Her father, dying from a lingering cancer, asked that she place these evergreens on Tamar Davidson's grave.

"Tamar Davidson," he whispered hoarsely, "is the mother you never knew." Trying to wipe away her father's tears, Kristin Davidson heard, for the first time, the true identity of her mother.

Kristin touched the cold headstone with her gloved hand, wiping away the accumulating snow. This strange snowfall had begun moments after her plane landed and now a total white-out obliterated the sky.

Tammy's parents, bundled in their warmest sweaters, approached the girl quietly. They were accustomed to seeing Tammy's fans try to gain a glimmer of understanding or hope by praying at her grave. The sounds of a Hebrew prayer softly reached their ears. They stood respectfully at a distance and listened until the young girl was finished. When Kristin turned around, she looked into the eyes of the grandparents she had never known and knew her father's last words were true. Tamar Davidson was her mother and these were her grandparents.

The sun found an opening in the unusual snow storm, illuminating Kristin as she leaned against the palm tree for support. Against the snow, the boughs of evergreen and blue ribbon glowed in the bright white light. A brilliant red cardinal, fluttered down and landed on Kristen's shoulder.

Tamar Davidson's parents fell to their knees, passionately embracing their granddaughter, who looked so much like her mother.

"Forgive my father," she said to them. "He died a tormented man. He had no idea of the pain he caused."

In the surreal light and snow, Kristen took the hands of her grandparents, lifted them up, and joyously raised their hands to her lips. The cardinal hovered above forming an apex to this triangle of love. The New Millennium had arrived; The Messianic Era had begun.

## My Sister's Closet

J opened the closet hoping to find some warmth. I needed a sweater. It was chilly up here on the 20th floor overlooking Central Park, and in this sleek Manhattan co-op, I couldn't find a snug corner to curl up in and read my book, so I needed a sweater.

The glass and chrome, polished, lacquered furniture was spotless and gleaming. There was not a fingerprint to be seen. I knew why. It was Tuesday. That was why! Elsie had just cleaned today. It always amazed me how one person could need a maid, but Elsie was in demand, and she faithfully cleaned and laundered for Ali twice a week. Not only was Elsie in demand, she was very trendy. Polish maids were in, much like the Louis Vuitton sweater I found carefully folded in the closet. I hesitated to remove it from its proper place and put it on. Everything looked so organized and perfect in her closet. Her closet was just like her life, only the best, organized and perfect. The Anne Taylor labels stared haughtily down at me from their lofty perches. I felt as if I was dreamily lost in the pages of Vogue magazine. I assumed a career woman needed a glamorous wardrobe.

As I wrapped the soft cashmere (I just knew it had to be cashmere) sweater around my shoulders, I eyed her tiny Gucci bag. I knew it contained the silver Elsa Peretti pen with which I had longingly watched her sign her Platinum American Express Card charges. As I sighed, I looked down at her sneakers neatly lined up in one corner, one pair for jogging, one for racquet ball, and the ones tucked a little farther back for tennis weekends in New Hampshire. All the names rang little bells in my mind. They were the best and the latest as advertised in this month's issue of Mademoiselle. The skiwear caught my eye next. I was a child again, lost in a candy store of fashion. The very latest in French insulated thinness and in my favorite color, pink, hung right before my eyes.

Envy was getting the best of me. Everything I ever dreamed of was right there in her closet. I closed the closet door feeling slightly moronic. She'd be home soon and find me lost in reverie inside her wardrobe.

I arrived here three days ago, needing my New York City fix of theater and museums and this time I actually remembered the order of the streets, Park, Lexington, Madison, or wait, is it Lexington, Madison, Park? Oh well, at any rate, I didn't have to stop and ask directions and my lucky guess turned out right. I never did get the order of the city streets straight. They were alien to me. Ali moved about them with such grace and ease.

I always felt like her little sister instead of the other way around, when I tripped along in my sneakers, beside her, while she artfully dodged taxis, joggers, and cyclists, while balancing perfectly in high heels, which I swear must have little built in radar detectors.

I got up out of her closet and walked over to her dainty kitchenette to make some tea. There was none. I had forgotten Ali had given up caffeine. I opened the fridge looking for something to nibble, but only saw what looked like a very expensive bottle of white wine. I dared not open it. Borrowing a sweater was one thing, drinking her wine before she even got home was quite another. Besides, she was probably saving it for a special date. God, what an exciting life. She really did have it all. I closed the fridge and saw a little magazine clipping. It was stuck on the refrigerator door with a tiny kitchen magnet shaped like a clock. On closer inspection, I realized it was a clock. A tiny digital clock that really worked. What next? I peered closer to read the article:

*Professional 34 Year Old Career Woman Who Enjoys The Excitement Of NYC And The Relaxation Of Country Weekends, Looking For Her Counterpart — Attractive Athletic Secure Male — Marriage And Family In Mind*

Just then Ali burst into the apartment with her mink coat (the product of this year's bonus check) casually slung over her arm.

"Hey Di, that sweater looks great on you. Why don't you keep it? It's last year's sample. We've got reservations at a great new restaurant, Pasta Galore. I've got to load up on those carbs. Running in a race tomorrow. Want a glass of white wine? I think there's some in the fridge. And hurry up and get dressed."

"I am dressed and there is white wine in the fridge, but that's about all there is. No carbs of any shape or form. What do you live on? Why don't you cook for yourself? You're a great cook. You always cook us delicious meals when you come up to New Hampshire for the weekend."

"Oh I love to cook for you and your brood. It's lots of fun! I never bother to cook for just myself. It's a waste. I'll experiment on your family."

"Experiment is the word Ali. Joe still talks about your hot dog soup."

"Ha! That was fresh escarole soup with imported Spanish sausage from Balduccis."

"I know what it was Ali and it was delicious. It just wasn't a stick to the ribs kind of dinner for teenagers. At least Joe was polite enough to wait until 9 o'clock before he ran out for chicken fingers."

"Gee, Di, talking about Joe, who would have ever thought my nephew would be a foot taller than me. He's a great kid, you're really lucky. And by the way, who was that friend of his who picked him up last weekend? Matt, I think Matt Feldman? Isn't he a lot older than Joe?"

"Yeah I think he's about six years older that Joe."

"What does he do for a living? He is out of school isn't he?"

"Oh no, Ali! That's robbing the cradle! Don't get any ideas! What would Joe say if I asked him to fix his aunt up with his buddy? He does have a good job with one of the major networks though, Hmm...."

"I'm only joking, Di. Only joking. Here let's have some wine. Do you see Doug around town?"

"Sure I do, Ali. Forget him."

"Oh I have, but I'm just curious...."

"Curiosity killed the cat, remember what mom used to say. It's only going to cause you grief."

"Well Daddy always said satisfaction brought him back, go on and spill. Well, what's he up to?"

"Oh I don't know."

"Yes you do, I can tell by the tone of your voice, out with it."

"Well I do see him around town every now and then with this one or that...."

"Mainly that one, am I right? I knew she was why he broke things off."

"Ali, this wine is great, let's drop the subject of Doug. What did you say it was Fooey Poose or Pooey Foose. Oh God, why did I have to take six years of Spanish. You sound so elegant when you speak French."

"The French Institute, remember, I work hard at it."

"Thanks a lot, I work hard at a lot of things too, I just never took French! Pour me some more wine, whatever it's called. Please. By the way, what's that junk on the fridge? Don't tell me you wrote that."

"O.K. I won't tell you I wrote that and what do you mean junk? Those four lines in New York Magazine cost me $450.00."

"Ali how could you? You never know what crackpot will answer those ads."

"What are you worried about? You've put ads in the paper for years renting out rooms to strangers."

"That's different."

"No it's not. Not at all, and what do you mean, how could I? How could I what, stoop so low. Don't be so smug. I suppose big sister would never do that! Well I did, and some of the responses weren't that bad. I really do get pretty lonely sometimes, but what would you know about that. Mother Theresa always has her doors open to every teenager within a 50-mile radius. No wonder your house is always such a mess. It took me one hour to find a vegetable peeler in your kitchen drawers. Everything was in there but kitchen utensils, a dog leash, used birthday candles, a broken 45 record, a lace glove, an old postcard, the list goes on and on."

"Everything is special in those drawers, and they are organized, you just have to understand what everything is and how much all those things mean to me. There is a special place for everything, and what do you mean a mess! At least it's not sterile like your apartment. It's lived in."

"Sterile! I pay Elsie a small fortune. It should be sterile! Pass me the wine, and while we're at it, what was that crack about robbing the cradle. It doesn't matter I suppose, that the merry widow is living with a guy ten years her junior, I suppose that's O.K."

"Ali that's different. He's a 34-year-old professional not a 26-year-old fresh out of college. Yea, it's O.K."

"Sure. It's always O.K. for you. You married and had a family and did it all perfectly!"

"Perfectly, look at you! You've got everything I've ever dreamed of. My wardrobe consists of your hand me ups. I look in your closet and I drool."

"You drool? You jerk, you don't think I envy you and your family? You've got it all!"

"I've got it all? I've got three sets of college tuitions and a multitude of other bills and a dead husband, and yes, I am probably playing nursemaid to that 34 year old."

"So for me it's wrong to even hint at getting involved with Joe's friend."

"It's different."

"It's not."

"Pour me some more wine!"

"It's all gone and I'm exhausted."

"I'm tired too, Ali, and I've got to go home. I'll never be able to find the FDR drive in the shape I'm in."

"Why go home and wait on everybody? Why don't you just stay in the city tonight?"

"I might just do that, suddenly I'm really hungry. Where did you say that new restaurant was?"

"Oh let's forget it. Why don't you wait here and I'll run out and get some more wine and incredible edibles from Balduccis."

"O. K. Ali that sounds great, and don't rush, if you can't find me when you get back, I'll just be curled up in your closet."

"What did you say?"

"Oh nothing Ali, it was really nothing."

○

Well, the years have come and gone. Many men have answered the various ads in our lives. Ali is now living with a man who has managed to find room to put his clothes in her closet. He has children from his first marriage who adore Ali. And me, well I married and divorced the younger man I was living with. He found my kitchen drawers totally devoid of meaning. Most days I spend writing, occasionally still reminiscing about the perfection of Ali's closet.

# A Life At The Movies

*Cinderella, Cinderella, night and day its Cinderella, wash the dishes, clean the table, scrub the laundry, clean the hall.* The words might not be exact, but it was Saturday afternoon and Daddy was taking me to the movies. It was probably my fifth excursion across the big bridge to Passaic, tightly gripping Daddy's hand, going to see my favorite movie, just one more time. Daddy serenaded me during the entire walk singing, Scallacadooza, Mitchakabooza, Bibbity-Bobbity-Boo. It was magic; he was mine, all mine, my very own handsome Prince Charming, just like in the movies.

For six happy years, I had my Daddy all to myself, until suddenly I had to share him with, not only one, but two baby sisters. Mom was dutifully left behind with the babies and I became my Daddy's princess for the day on Saturdays. It was no surprise the movie I kept begging to see was *Cinderella*. I had Prince Charming in my pocket for the day. It was quite some time before I realized my Daddy was not the man who was supposed to sweep me off my feet and lead me to happy for ever and after. Quite some time before I realized I had to do that for myself.

So there I sat in the plush, purple, velvet seat, my royal throne, dining on the regal treats of chocolate covered bon-bons. I sat snug and secure, watching Cinderella cook and clean and talk to her animals. Every time I returned home, I begged mom to wrap my hair in a kerchief when we cleaned house, just like Cinderella wore her hair in the movies. I've never outgrown that habit, or the pearls Daddy gave me for my first communion. Birds could have strung them around my neck, just like in the movie. I was beautiful, virginal, white and pure then, convinced that when you wish upon a star, your dreams do come true.

But the gentle fifties were coming to an end. Women of a certain age knew the *Cinderella Complex* was no work of fiction. We were raised by mothers who elevated our Daddies, in their handsome World War II uniforms, to princely levels. I recognized myself with glaring clarity. I baked my first cake for Daddy and ironed my first shirt. Love and passion intermixed with laundry and dusting coloring every chore.

The movie, *Bambi*, soon became part of our repertoire, as well as *Snow White* and *Dumbo*. Mom still got Saturday afternoons off, something I now really appreciate. I still see the animated figures prancing in my head. Wasn't it only yesterday, I quieted my baby sister's fears as she watched the forest fire flash across the screen in *Bambi*? I can still hear Bambi's father telling him, "Man, Bambi, man did this," or is it my father telling me years later, "Man, Dianalee, man caused this," as the latest causality figures from the Vietnam War flashed across the TV screen?

The image of that animated forest fire soon became transposed with the image of flags burning; draft cards burning; the spirit of youth inflamed. Images of the sixties, as if on a screen, flash through my mind. Was my Daddy putting my pearls tenderly around my neck or was it his substitute, the new love of my life, Joe, going through the same motions, before our prom? I wasn't ironing or cleaning or baking for Joe. We were joining our arms and protesting the war; a war even my father, the World War II hero, whispered was unjust.

Movies took on another fascinating twist in the sixties; I realized they could be comfortably viewed from the front seat, I did say front seat, of a Chevy convertible with my new Prince charming hugging me securely. The screen blazed in the sixties, and so did I. Unfortunately, drive-in movies were strictly forbidden! They were right up there, sub-topic A, under honor thy father and thy mother. A: Do not ever go to a drive-in movie. But, hey, it was the sixties. Honor was a word with lots of flexibility. We were honoring our country by burning flags, draft cards and bras. Off we went every weekend until that night when flames spread across the screen again. Napalm was being sprayed, babies were burning and dying, and the Capital Theater, where I was supposed to be, had burnt down to the ground. Arson was suspected.

"How was the movie?" The question had icicles hanging with its tone. I should have known something was very wrong, but I really did see a movie. I went on to describe the film, we had barely seen at the drive-in, in stunning detail. It never occurred to me that the sirens going off in my head were from anything other than ecstasy. I finally finished with a flourish. "It was just fabulous!" I looked around; parental stares of betrayal surrounded me.

"We'll discuss this in the morning," was the comment I hoped for. After a lifetime of waiting, it was said. This gave me time to think. I averted my eyes from Daddy, my first Prince Charming, and walked out the door to say goodbye to Joe, his number 1 substitute.

We didn't say goodbye. We clung to each other like desperate puppies seeking the warmth of a vacated womb. These were turbulent times. I stood caught between two Prince Charmings. Joe and I talked most of the night on my front porch, my parents somehow uncharacteristically not interfering. We made many decisions that night. We would leave tomorrow, elope and have a child very soon. Exemption was a word filled with passion; I love yous on our lips, college would have to wait. The war was becoming ugly. Canada began to look promising to Joe. If that was what he wanted, so did I. With one last look at his low draft card number, we lit a match, watched the smoke curl, and headed to Maryland. Within 24 hours I would be his Mrs., just like that, Bibbity-Bobbity-Boo. It was magic, just like in the movies.

Now with terror on the screens, I see those times of my life like movie stills; moments of my life at the movies. The final cut, the vision imbedded in my brain, is of an empty theater. All of the purple plush seats are empty, old, and shabby. I see my parents on life's big screen, watching the horrors of the war, and the burnt out rubble of the Capital Theater on their small black and white TV. They have realized their oldest daughter, Dianalee, has gone and their world will be forever changed. In this last frame my father always puts his head in his hands and weeps, while my mother silently stares, stoically ahead, into the future. Bambi's father comes back on the screen and echoes, "Man, Bambi, man has done this."

That imagined scene, I play over and over again. It was a turning point for me, a turning point in my life at the movies.

# Church Bells Will Ring

I am flying back home from Miami, serenely gazing out at the billowing white fluff below me, an acute reminder of why I am traveling on a cloud. These cumulus wonders remind me of the armful of diaphanous flowing bridal veil my daughter and I have just safely placed in a friend's Miami home. We have decided, my daughter and I, that her new home is much too chaotic and dusty to house this treasure. I am careful not to use the word dirty; they are after all in the midst of construction. I am learning to play a new role, mother-in-law. My baby is getting married in three weeks. Ah weddings....

I smile as I think back to my own wedding over twenty-six years ago. A small exciting affair. A '57 Chevy. A car radio playing, "Hey Paul, I want to marry you. Hey, hey, Paula, I want to marry you too," and a thirteen state alarm out for my beloved and me. Abducting a minor was a serious charge, although as I snuggled tightly against Joe's slender body, the wind from the convertible in our faces, I didn't feel very abducted at all. Crazy kids; we eloped. Crazier still it lasted. It lasted for a long time. Now the only sound of Paula ringing in my ears is that of my fiancé's ex-wife. "Hey, hey, Paula, are the dogs doing well?" "Hey, hey Bob, yes, but they still love you too." My first husband is gone, dead, deceased and like my daughter, I too am embarking on a new life, complete with the shared custody of eight Siberian huskies. Ah divorce....

I glance out my window again. We are flying above water that appears clear, tranquil and smooth, but we are flying high. I am sure, upon closer inspection, you would be able to see the waves and the choppiness and begin to imagine what lurks in the depths. Marriage can be like that. An apparent smooth surface, a formal joining, but take a closer look and you can see the undertow creating waves. You must really dive to the depths, with protective gear of course, to see and appreciate the true beauty.

At this point, I choose to view my daughter's approaching marriage from my present airborne height through sunshine and cloud like bridal veils. A marriage that will be as smooth as the imported silk of her wedding gown. But I know. I know there will be waves in their marriage. I only hope Filly and Fred have the courage to explore the depths.

Courage. We will all need courage to begin our new lives. I am a widow with two grown children, marrying a man ten years my junior, with eight Siberian huskies, an ex-wife, and a father who is a prominent Rabbi. I will have many new depths to explore. I am in unknown territory. Scuba diving was easy by comparison. Now, I will have no oxygen tank to keep the air clear and my heart free. No protective gear to guide my free mind and spirit. I fear I will need more than fins to keep me afloat. But I love a challenge; it is in my blood.

My daughter has always admired my free spirit and delighted in tales of my first wedding. She grew up with the dreamy notion she would be married, barefoot, on the beach in front of our Mexican island home. Secretly. Telling everyone only after it was done and the sun had set. But there were too many unexpected sunsets. Her dad died and she followed the sun that he loved and moved to Miami (which is why I sit here writing now in this DC10). It is in Miami, while attempting to pursue her Master's, that she met Freddy and fell in love.

"Hi Mom...I don't think I'll be coming home for Christmas."

"It's OK, Babe" (ever cautious since being widowed not to appear lonely). "What's up, where will you be spending the day?"

"Oh probably with Uncle John and Aunt Helen, and, oh ,by the way, I got this beautiful ring last week from a friend."

*And, oh, by the way...* My mind was racing but I maintained my cool.

"Oh really, what kind?"

"A diamond ring, Mom." Then there is total silence as my cool slips away.

"Are you engaged?" Or married, I thought, as the beach scene flashed through my mind.

"Oh, no, Mom, we're just real good friends. I can't wait for you to meet Freddie in January."

And meet Freddie we did, my soon to be son-in-law, in January almost exactly two years ago. Ah Freddie....

I really don't know what I expected, since my family has never been one to follow any norms. There was no set mode for my daughter to follow in her choice of a husband. With our proper Catholic upbringing, the women in my family have managed to embrace the world in their arms, or at least the male representatives of all the world's major religions. My middle sister is happily married to a Japanese gentleman and is content mothering my exotic niece. I myself am taking the plunge into Judaism, so as one might guess, my new son-in-law to be is Arabic. Ah life....

With much more than a little trepidation, my fiancé and I went down to Miami in January and greeted Filly and her dark mysterious friend. Within moments of our arrival, just seconds off the runway, they joyously told us of their engagement and of the party in their honor we were to attend that evening. Our own little private summit meeting. What joy! What worry! For nothing! The evening turned out to be a lovely affair although it resembled an Arab-Israeli peace conference, right out of Marakesh. My daughter's new father-in-law, to be (what will he be to me?) spent much of the evening proclaiming to my fiancé the close association he held with the Israelis. I was beginning to feel very neglected.

"Hey guys," I wanted to yell. "Remember me. I'm the mother of the bride; he's only my fiancé. Impress me. Are you close with Polish Catholics?" No one seemed to care. I was in another world, and it wasn't Miami. I was totally out of my element. I wanted to run away and take my baby with me. Ah motherhood....

Through all this, my baby and her sweetie smiled and hugged and kissed and called each other "Honey Bunny." My son rolled his eyes and choked back laughter. He was witnessing a new scene. He was watching his sister in love. Seated between us was Freddies grandmother, all sweetness and light, and though her command of English was really quite limited, she managed to convey this message to us, "In my day, you no touch until you're married." Now this dear sweet little old lady knew Freddie and Filly were living together and had already purchased their first home. She was also told that Bob and I live together as well. Her point was well taken in the space of silence that followed.

Now, this little piece of information might seem trivial, but it was one of the sharks lurking beneath all this tranquility. Very shortly after I mailed a mountain of invitations to Filly and Freddie's wedding (no she did not decide to get quietly married on the beach, a subject I will elaborate on later), I received a poison pen letter from my own dear mother. I guess the trauma of my own elopement was preferable to the fact her granddaughter had decided to have a big white wedding while living in "sin" with the man she had chosen to marry.

"But why not!" the letter went on to exclaim. "Look at the example her mother is setting, and her aunt." Now why she chose to throw my sister in for good measure I'll never know. It just didn't seem fair. Just because my baby sister is living with another Jewish orthodontist, my fiancé's profession as well, who also happens to bear a striking resemblance to my Bob, shouldn't give her cause to lump the two situations together. This is not grounds for wrath. In fact she should be laughing. Two sisters still able to communicate and love each other while dating the two competing Jewish orthodontists in Fairfield County is no small coup. I choose to try and ignore my mother's blast, but I am hurt. Happiness should be enough and we have plenty of that. The rest is sheer nonsense.

I get up now to use the lavatory and the captain immediately flashes the fasten seat belt sign on, and announces, "All those who are in the aisle please return to your seats and fasten your seat belts. We will be experiencing some turbulence." The voice of authority has spoken. What an underestimate, in both cases. I return to my seat feeling chastised, and insecure, much as I did when I had read my mother's letter, and just for doing what comes naturally.

Well there was plenty of turbulence. In panic I thought of my son. He would be left all alone. He hadn't yet found that perfect partner for life, and then I began to laugh. The only one, I might add, laughing while the plane plunged and plummeted and then gained steady air space once again. Who will he share his life with? Who could possibly add to our growing ethnic diversity? An American Indian? Perhaps, an Eskimo? Visions of these imaginary wedding ceremonies floated in my brain as the lightning flashed outside my window and I continued to giggle. The flight attendant asked me if I was OK. I turned around laughing and told her there are no Wasps. She looked around, gave me a blanket and a pillow and said the turbulence should soon be over, while patting my shoulder in an understanding manner. I don't think she understood. I was not speaking of bugs but of people. There are no white Anglo Saxon Protestants in our family to give us blond babies. If my son does not meet and fall in love with exactly such a girl, after being raised in Darien, CT, then it is just not meant to be. Ah daydreams....

The turbulence does seem to stop, but we are flying much lower now and not over water. Land stretches out below us. I can see the hub of a city with its tall buildings and all the smaller ones radiating out from the center. The tall office buildings become smaller ones. Closely knit homes then follow opening up to freer expanses with homes and pools, commonly called the suburbs. The suburbs gently slide into beautiful green rolling plains and I am lost in my daydreams again. I am galloping across the open plains on my beloved Andrew's back. Andrew is my horse and I suddenly miss him very much. He has been a constant in my life. I am lost in time and place and long to throw my arms around his neck and feel his warmth but it is the airplane blanket that I wake up hugging.

The scene below, actually everything I see, reminds me of Filly and Freddie's upcoming wedding. Like this unknown city below me, it has grown. It is spreading; creating a life of its own. I remember when Filly first told me she and Freddie had decided not to have a small quiet intimate wedding. I was elated. Having never had a big wedding of my own, now I was to be the mother of the bride. Visions of sugarplums twirled in my head and I wanted this wedding to be a fairy tale dream come true.

Miami. Of course the wedding would be in Miami. The search began. Friends offered their home on the water and it was our first choice, but after trying to determine where we would seat everyone we decided it was too small. In retrospect, it might have been smart to limit the space since our final choice, Viscaya, an opulent old mansion on Biscayne Bay, had the capacity to seat a small army, which we eventually did. And yes, this is where the reception will finally take place, Viscaya Gardens, good enough for the Pope and our President to meet, good enough for my only daughter. Of course we chose the same caterer who proudly told us he had served the Pope and President at the summit. This proved to be the first step in an embryonic cycle of planning a wedding. Having now leased out all this space, we felt compelled to fill it with more guests ($$) and more musicians ($$) and more flowers ($$) and more photographers ($$) and more videographers ($$), (twentieth century tech), and a huge bridal party ($$). The ands continue to pour down upon us and the wedding is only three weeks away. I stare in amazement as the response cards are delivered each day to my doorstep. People we assumed would never make the trip are coming from the four corners of the earth, thrilled to be invited, joyous to share this day with us. Ah weddings.

Well, almost everyone is joyous, except my mother. "Why? Why must this wedding be held in Miami? She is my first granddaughter to be married and I may never live to see the other one married. You've destroyed me! You've shunned my side of the family; no one can come!" (That's what you think, I mused. Look at the responses on my doorstep). Now I honestly think Miami is a lovely place to be in March and proceeded to tell my Mom so. How silly I was to voice an opinion. The guilt came on even stronger. "We get the worst snowstorms up north in March and we'll never get to the airport. You could have at least made it in April." There was no correct thing for me to say or do. It was obvious no matter what I said it would be construed as a plot to keep her from her granddaughter's wedding. I tried to be patient and continued to listen. "The bride should be married in her mother's house." It seemed my Mom had her own preconceived notion of how Filly's wedding should be planned.

I staunchly tried to defend my daughter. "Miami is her home now, Mom. She hasn't lived here in Darien for two years and besides it is what she wants. That's what's really important!"

"It doesn't matter what she wants." (I don't understand this comment at all and can't believe it is my mother speaking. Do weddings cause everyone to become irrational?) "She should be married in your home."

The verbal barrage continued but I staunchly defended my daughter's decision. That is until December, the month Filly and Freddie picked up and moved to El Paso, Texas. I watched all my lovely excuses go down the drain and waited (not for too long) for the next phone call.

It came, as I had expected. "I thought Filly loved Miami and it was her home." My mother's voice on the other end of the line was not merely asking a question. This was going to be an inquisition. "I received a birthday card today from Filly and Freddie and she tells me they have moved to Texas." My mind begins to race trying to come up with a plausible explanation.

Gritting my teeth and grimacing, I begin to speak into the smoking telephone. "It is their home, Mom. They've bought a charming house and in three or four years (or more), after their new business gets off the ground they may even be living in it. They do intend to come back for the wedding though." It sounded like a lame explanation even to my own ears. "They will be in Miami for the whole month of March." I try to blank out the next onslaught. I can tell my mother is furious. When I hang up the phone, I am ready to strangle everyone, bride, groom, grandparents, etc., but it is poor Bob who is standing there next to me, and it is at him that I snap. He looks hurt and injured and I realize how much I love him. I am quick to apologize. He is quick to accept. He always understands. Ah love....

When we started making plans for this wedding, I made myself one big promise. No lost tempers, no family squabbles; all that could safely be avoided. I had watched too many weddings bring out the worst in the meekest and gentlest old aunts. With all my best intentions it seems this is an inevitable part of all weddings. Maybe it is a tradition. If the bride and groom can stand the stress, they will live happily ever after. Everyone, it seems, is complaining about something. Everyone, that is, except Filly and her Freddie. They are isolated in El Paso, blissful, alone, with an unpublished telephone number. I have visions of moving the wedding to Cincinnati or some other central city. It will then become a very small and very private affair. I may not even tell the bride and groom. Tell no one. Ah fantasy....

The air in the airplane is getting stuffy. I think I need to turn on the airflow or maybe I'll press the help button and call the flight attendant. I wonder if she would listen to the wedding woes. Not a very great idea.

People are already looking at me strangely, the woman laughing during the turbulence and talking about bugs. I could try to nap, but my mind is full of lists and more lists to remind me of lists. Lists to remind me of all the things I must accomplish in three weeks. Lists. There are more invitations to send out. (How could I have possibly forgotten Filly's Godmother? Maybe because I haven't seen her in ten years. That's a good enough reason in my book.) I still need more fittings for my dress to reach perfection. Right now it could house two of me, which is what I need right now, at least. Several of me. One to be the mother of the bride, one to be Joe's mom, one to be an understanding daughter (even after all those phone calls), one to be a professional, to pay for this extravaganza, and one to study (through all this I am trying to pursue my Masters), and last but not least, one to be Bob's fiancée, because through all this there is always Bob.

Bob and I are trying to start a new life, selling my home, his condo, buying one that is ours. Anyone who has ever tried to buy and sell a home and coordinate the efforts will automatically realize that to do this only three weeks before my daughter's wedding borders on lunacy. We are pulling up carpets and memories, painting walls and breaking down barriers. We are running in circles yet encircling each other every night as we collapse in exhaustion, laughter and sometimes tears. It is a time of waiting. Waiting for the wedding, waiting for our mortgage to be approved, waiting for my dress to finally fit and waiting to move into our new home; waiting to build our own memories.

Old memories await us in every closet we open. Old photographs of my first wedding bear no resemblance to the ball we are planning. Pictures of Bob's first wedding do. I imagine it was complete with all the frustrations and joys I am now experiencing as I plan Filly's wedding. I feel green and not only with inexperience. I also feel something new.

I look at pictures of Bob and his first wife. She seemed to be his perfect mate. She is pretty, educated (Ph.D.), younger than he (perfect for childbearing), Jewish, and above all else, applauded by his parents. A perfect ten for marriage material. I feel a sting of hurt. It was three long years before Bob's family began speaking to him after we moved in together. I ask him if he is sure that I am the person he wants. (I must have asked this question a hundred times in five years.) He smiles and tells me he has never been so in love. Neither have I. This is a mature romance. We can now sit back and giggle childishly, when we think of our first date with my two teenage children in tow and the fact that someone asked Filly if she was dating Bob. After my laughter my stomach does a little flip-flop. I remember her answer,

"No he's my Mom's, all Mom's." What am I doing marrying a younger man? Ah, self doubt....

My first marriage, on the other hand, was performed somewhere in Maryland (right across the state line if my memory serves me right), no waiting, no blood tests, nobody there. I remember being young and in love and terrified to go back home and face the music and my parents. We, of course, finally did call both sets of parents and were urged to come back home to the tune of lots of tears and hysteria. I was a stigma to my mother; how could she face her friends? Was I pregnant? Probably by now. There was no such thing as the pill. While our parents wailed, we attained folk hero status with our friends. The romantic duo; the first to tie the knot, and the youngest, and to the chagrin of many parents, not the last. Our little adventure seemed to start a trend. Life again assumed a routine. Joe went back to his second year of college, and yes, I was pregnant. Our life together had begun. Cashless! Ah, young love....

My new marriage will be quiet, once again, performed by a Justice of the Peace, unless of course, we can find a Rabbi on the east coast who does not know Bob's father and is willing to perform this dastardly deed. We dream of having our wedding on a snow-covered mountain in Vermont, near the ski home we purchased together last year, but I suspect the snow will be long gone before we have some time to ourselves and the flurries of Filly's wedding have settled. We are quite a team. We live together, work together and play together. We will begin this new marriage without the money problems we had both experienced when we had started our firsts. It is a nice feeling, though very short-lived. Filly's wedding, coming into full bloom will keep us humble. The bills are beginning to pour in. Ah weddings....

The plane is beginning its final descent. I will be home shortly. The view below me is crystal clear, much like hindsight. We are in the process of landing, flying along the coast. The vast expanses of blue ocean spill into many sparkling bays and then into wide green rivers surrounded by foliage. The rivers narrow off into tiny tributaries then into streams and then thin out until they completely disappear, all the nourishing water entirely engulfed by densely populated land.

My first marriage was like that. Open and vast and crystal clear until it became long and narrow and smothered by the problems leading up to the divorce. It hurts me, even now, to think of my marriage in terms of the pain. It is hard for me to remember the divorce. I am his widow. The ink on the divorce papers had not even dried when all of a sudden he was dead. I mourned as his widow. I accepted the bouquet of icy white roses he had sent me. Ironically they where delivered the day after he died. He died while still trying to celebrate what would have been our 23rd wedding anniversary. He was dead, my husband. My companion since the age of twelve. My champion. My grown kids and I looked up occasionally from our grief to see his young girlfriend standing beside his coffin. Did she ever shed a tear? Had they even begun to explore the depths of their relationship? Did she really love him? I am his widow. I will always be his widow. The plane is about to land. I love to fly and I love weddings; both give me time to pause and reflect. Ah life….

My toes are pink and puckered and par-boiled. The mother of the bride is having a pedicure. Why, I'm still not sure. I am not wearing open toe sandals to the wedding or to the rehearsal dinner and I am reasonably sure even if I was, no one would be paying much attention to my feet. Maybe I am here for the refuge. Actually, I am certain that is exactly why I am here, away from the constantly ringing telephone. The wedding is now less than two weeks away. I dread the thought of what my phone bill will be, but whatever it is, it will be one tenth of Filly's. She is now calling from Miami, yes she is back in Miami, at least ten times a day.

"Mom, why aren't you calling me anymore?" she laments. I think to myself that I can't honestly think of anything constructive to say when only fifteen minutes have elapsed since her last phone call. We really should have installed a Watts line between Miami and Darien. I am sure it would have been cost effective. I am trying to maintain a sense of calm to ensure Filly stays calm. It is proving to be very hard work. Only yesterday I was besieged by two crying hysterical phone calls, both from the women I love the most in my life; both of whom I want to see happy. My mother called first in tears, "If this wedding had been in Connecticut, I would have bought a new dress." Of course I feel a twinge of guilt and then angry frustration. I almost begged my mom to come up here with my sister and me to have a gown made; now ten days before the wedding she is still handing me this guilt trip.

"You can still go out and buy one Mom," I offer as I try to be somewhat rational.

"No, it's too late now. I don't want to talk about it."

This sounds like a wonderful idea to me, but mom did continue to talk about it for at least another ten minutes. I suspect she is feeling a little sorry for herself. We did not change the wedding plans when she expressed her wrath and now the only one she is punishing is herself. I feel hurt and helpless but it was her choice.

Next phone call. "MOM, I tried my wedding gown on again and it falls off my shoulders." Hysterically now, "What am I going to do? I hate the bra they sold me with it. My boobs fall out and it feels like a vise. MOM help!"

"Filly, stay calm. All you have to do is take it back to the store and have them fix it." I was trying to maintain a calm even I didn't feel.

"Oh Mom, I can't go by myself. I wish you were here." The thought occurs to me I should fly down to Miami and help Filly, just as the thought occurred to me I should drive down to New Jersey to help my mom find a dress, but I am quickly realizing that I am not superwoman.

"Filly, you'll do just fine. Ask Mirtha to go with you. She'll be even better than me; she can argue with them in Spanish."

"Oh Mom, what a great idea, I'll call you later." Click. Ten minutes later the phone rings again.

"Mom, she'll come. That was a great idea, and oh by the way, I need another check for $2,000.00 for the florist, for the deposit. Bye!"

My heart sinks a little. Actually it sinks a lot. This wedding is going to cost a great deal more than we had anticipated, but I have heard all weddings do. It comes as no consolation. I elect not to tell Filly, at this time, I have just seen one of her bridesmaid's gowns and it is not lined with the correct color. I decide to casually mention she should call Priscilla (who is notoriously late with everything), and see how her gown is coming along. I hang up feeling exhausted and it is only 8:30 in the morning. I await the next phone call. It comes quickly. It is Priscilla asking me urgently if I have any more of the fabric left from the gowns. She will be right over (from Queens) to meet her mother (from upstate Connecticut) to try on her dress (which is lined with the wrong color) for the first time. I am sure Filly is at home, again in tears. Ah patience....

The hubbub of the last few days has taken my mind off very serious conversations I have had with Filly and Freddie over the past few weeks. Divorce does not make wedding seating arrangements easy. Who sits where becomes as important as NATO defense. Freddie's parents are divorced (as well) and both are remarried. Can the front row of the groom's side hold all that reorganization or do we split them up, but then, who deserves the front pew? It is a dilemma not worth worrying about. We decide to seat them all in the front and everyone is too happy to move. Sounds very good in theory. Now for the bride's side. Bob and I will sit in the first pew, I hope alongside my first husband's parents, and our dear friends, who have been like parents to Filly in Miami, will join us there also. Filly's Grandpa Joe is giving her away and they really deserve this place of honor. Also in the first row will be my Mom, who I hope will be crying with joy not with the fact she hasn't purchased a new dress and the fact the wedding is here in Miami. It will be an interesting combination of people. My sister, Ali, has promised to stay with Filly till the last moment so she will have to fend for herself, although I would prefer to have her at my other side. I used to worry about crying at Filly's wedding since it is one of the things I do easily and frequently, but if we pull all this off in a relatively calm manner, I believe I will be so relieved, I will just give her one big thumbs up sign as she proceeds down the aisle. We are counting down and all systems are go.

Filly and Freddie have spoken to me a lot about divorce. Both kids (they are still kids in my eyes) have gone through it first-hand. Both vow they are marrying for life, never again wanting to experience the pain and separation divorce brings to every family member it touches. I know in my heart they mean every word they are saying but I can't help but cross my fingers and pray a little. I thought my first marriage was for life. I hope my second one will be. Marriage requires lots of little prayers. I agree with the kids wholeheartedly. Once again, I am marrying for life. I do take marriage seriously, but I've been there. The little prayers I utter include many for Bob and myself. I smile at the kids and try to break the solemnity of the conversation.

"Well kids, this wedding is on me. If you do it again Filly, you're on your own." (I am joking, but not really.) They both look at me and they are not laughing. They look like little wounded puppies. This will be the one and only wedding for both of them. I smile and say another little prayer.

I am a pray-er. By that I mean I talk to God a lot. I have always considered myself a very spiritual person though not a very religious one (if you consider organized religion the only religion). I believe we all pray to the same God, we just do it in a variety of different ways. We are still having a difficult time in finding a Rabbi willing to marry a prominent Rabbi's son and his outspoken bride-to-be. I insist on stating my true beliefs. When Filly's wedding is over, we will start the search again. Rabbis in the tri-state area are running out of excuses not to marry us. We shall see. Ah perseverance….

The problem of divorce almost caused us to have two rehearsal dinners. Freddie's mom and dad were both planning two separate affairs. But that problem has been amiably solved. Freddie's Dad will give the dinner the night before the wedding. In true Arabic fashion it is to be replete with belly dancers. My mother will have much more to be unhappy with; her dress will never cross her mind.

Inwardly I am laughing to myself. It will be some wedding! Christians, Buddhists and Jews all dancing under one big umbrella of happiness, my daughter's wedding. We really should be doing our own Coca-Cola commercial and try to "Teach the world to sing in perfect harmony." Well, that's what we'll hope for anyway. Perfect harmony or something at least close.

It is interesting that I approach this stage of my life confronting many of the same issues my daughter now faces. I never imagined this would be the case. She and Freddie work together as Bob and I do. They have lived together and bought a home together before they were married as Bob and I have done. They have finally decided to get married as Bob and I have. (Well not exactly as we have; there will be vast differences in the celebrations.) They are also facing an unknown future together. They are trusting and loving and trying to attain that perfect balance of knowing and loving another human being.

Well, my pedicure is done and my time of peace and quiet is finished. Bob and I want to clean the basement this weekend. Realtors will be pouring through the house with a fine-tooth comb. It is a good time for hard work. Bob and I will continue to fall asleep every night in each other's arms, exhausted. Ah love....

And now to the basement. All our earthly possessions, with which we have any strange attachment and some of which we have no inkling why we are keeping, are now in the basement. There is not even a clear pathway to walk through and in just several days it must be as immaculate as the rest of the house, ready for the white glove realtor test. We are playing beat the clock. We have one day and one day only to accomplish this miracle. Every cherished book I own must be boxed (and I do cherish all my books). Bob and my son Joe are having a hard time understanding why it is necessary for me to keep my 7th grade history book but it is my fetish, so they continue to box. I cannot bear to part with any book I have ever owned. I'm sure it dates back to my years of walking to the library (yes through snow and rain and sleet) to take out my treasured reading material. (And no, I didn't read by candlelight.)

Somewhere in the basement, amid the turmoil, it occurs to Bob and me that this is the weekend we thought we might slip away and get married. The weekend before THE wedding was supposed to be ours. In our subterranean hideaway, covered with dust, and holding dirty wet rags we are quite the romantic couple! We have only three precious hours left to clean and there is no time for sentiment. The first realtor is coming at three o'clock. We box faster and scrub harder. Marriage for us will have to wait.

At three o'clock, on the nose, the doorbell rings. I have barely made it out of the shower. Bob, on the other hand, has to forsake his. We are off to Vermont, not Miami. In retrospect, this was a wonderful idea despite my growing anxiety that I should already be in Miami with my Filly. A trip to Vermont, the weekend before the wedding, (though not for our own wedding as we had envisioned) will be a time to relax (heaven knows we need it), to regroup our thoughts and to ski until exhaustion sets in. I am sure it will take my mind off (well not entirely) the upcoming wedding. And it does. Ah fresh powder….

Vermont is pure bliss. There are no clouds in the dazzling blue sky. There is perfect snow and the temperature hovering near forty-five degrees. Skiing in just a sweater and jeans, in perfect conditions, brings us as close to heaven as we can possibly imagine. The world seems crystal clear and radiant. Bob stops me at the top of the mountain to tell me how much he loves me; it is exactly how I feel about him. It seems we have the whole mountain to ourselves and I have never been happier or for the moment more relaxed. Our marriage will come eventually, as soon as we find the time. It is becoming less and less important. This moment is special and romantic; the kind of moment a man should propose marriage. As I tell Bob this we both grin from ear to ear with the memory of the night he really did propose. Romantic it was not. A midwinter nightmare, really. With a ready, set, go, we decide to race down the mountain, laughing in our solitude with the memory.

We had been living together for over three years when Bob and I decided to go our separate ways. Like two grown-up rational adults we discussed our differences (we don't even make a bed the same way) and decided they were too numerous. It was time to move on. The fact was now working in Bob's office, as his office manager, complicated matters somewhat, but we were mature. I would stay until I found something else and had trained my replacement. We tried to be mature and unemotional; what a joke. We should have known better.

We didn't time things well. In fact, we didn't time them at all. Sometimes you just say things when they have to be said. All this was said two days before our gala office party. I knew instinctively I should be at this party. It would be the best and the brightest, the culmination of five years of hard work, on both our parts; but it would find us for the first time, in that many years, not together. With all our mature and rational thinking, the first day together at the office, after our momentous decision, brought a tension that was snappable. I was beginning to inhale and exhale very slowly (you would think I was practicing Lamaze breathing) to get through the day. I decided it was going to be too much of a strain on me to go through with this party and I decided to tell Bob just that. I pulled myself up tall and all five feet four inches of me stood firm while my stomach housed a flying circus. My prepared speech flew out of my brain and somewhere into the atmosphere.

"I really don't think I can go to the party this evening," was all I managed to stammer through quivering lips. "Maybe I'll just make an appearance and leave early. I'll think of some excuse."

Bob appeared quite in control. "No, I think you should be there for the whole evening. The staff knows it is required and you ARE the office manager. I really didn't think it would feel this awful either. I'm really sorry." His controlled manner was beginning to irritate me and helped to stop my quivering lips and calm the trapeze act going on in my stomach.

"I'm pretty sorry too. This is not what I had expected. I think you have to take this. It's my resignation." I felt smug. I could be just as controlled as he was.

But the comment seemed ridiculous and with it I handed the man I love a silly short typed note that read, "Due to an emotional conflict, I can no longer stay in your employment."

All was said and done. It seemed like such an understatement. Why did we do this now? Why did we arrive at this decision just days before this party? This party that we inaugurated five years ago as a small gathering for referring doctors was now a tradition for some 200, associates, wives and staffs included. I had to leave quickly. My rationale was beginning to slip.

Without taking another moment to look into Bob's eyes, I turned quickly with tears in mine and left for the damn party. He wanted me to go and I would. My hands were shaking on the steering wheel and I could not believe I was going all alone. Knowing soon I would be in the company of friends and business associates, as well as my son and all his friends, I forced myself to maintain my composure but it was not easy. Fury was taking over! What nerve he had telling me I had to go. I vowed not only not to cry but also to stay the whole evening and have one grand time. I surprised even myself. I did!

The office grapevine had done its job and it was apparent to some people at the party that I was fair game. By the end of the evening I had a date for Friday night and one for New Year's Eve. I danced and I danced, on and on. I knew if I stopped, I'd crumble and cry because as I danced, my eyes never once left Bob. God did I love him!

The party started to break up and several people offered me a ride home. I refused. I really wanted to be alone and I meant it. A well-meaning gentleman friend followed me out to my car, ignoring all my protestations. "You really shouldn't be alone tonight, I know what you're going through." (Sure I thought to myself. Do I look like I was born yesterday?)

"No," I repeated, as I removed his arm from around my shoulder, "I really want to be alone." And I did. As soon as I wrestled my way free and into the safety of my car I started to cry. I didn't feel grown-up and I didn't feel rational. I didn't know what I felt, but it wasn't what I had expected.

I drove toward home but decided I didn't want to walk in the door and have my son see me with red puffy swollen eyes and in this wrecked emotional state. As if by magic, my car switched direction and I headed to the home of a dear friend. When she answered the door she thought I was laughing hysterically. As it soon became apparent this was not the case, she ushered me upstairs like a good Mommy and put me to sleep in her bed with her fourteen-year-old niece's nightshirt. She kept brushing my hair and soothing my face until I stopped crying and began laughing upon observation of my situation. The front of the T-shirt I was now wearing had a comic book heroine, with big teardrops falling on her cheeks, crying about a lost love. Laughing and sniffling I fell sound asleep.

Somewhere around 2:30 in the morning I awoke with a start. The house was strange and quiet and it took me a moment to remember where I was. Everyone was asleep. I wanted to go home. If Joe had gone straight home after the party, by now he would be worried about my whereabouts. Even if he wasn't home, my dogs had to be let out. It's not easy being a responsible adult. I didn't have time for this folly. I had not been home since seven o'clock this morning. Trying to be as quiet as I could, I slipped on my high heels, rolled my clothes into a ball and tiptoed out of the house to my car. I prayed that my son was either not yet home or sound asleep. I did not want to offer an explanation on why I was coming home with nothing more on than a comic book T shirt and high heels, with my clothing tucked neatly under my arm. I pulled into my driveway and not only was every light on in the house, but my son, Bob and some friends were all standing in the front hall frantically looking out for my arrival. I put the car savagely into reverse (something that would later cost me quite a few dollars in repair bills) and backed out in a rage! I was angry and confused! I wanted to go home, to my home, but how could I? My house was occupied by the enemy. I drove around the block and realized the ridiculousness of the situation. I couldn't drive back to May's house; the door would surely be locked and I wasn't about to wake up the whole family once again. I couldn't drive around all night. I had passed one police car and the thought of getting pulled over in my unique attire was not appealing. I turned the corner and headed for home. The party was over.

I tried to look dignified as I walked to my front door but I could imagine what I must look like. Bob stood at the front door looking haggard and worried and much older than his thirty-six years.

"Don't say a word. Don't tell me a thing. I don't want to know where you've been. Just listen." He started talking so fast I didn't have time to begin my explanation. I only wanted to go up the stairs and go to sleep. "I want to spend the rest of my life with you," he continued. "These have been the two most miserable days of my whole life. I want you to be my wife."

My son listened to this proposal while eyeing me up and down and shouted, "Where the hell have you been?" ignoring the conversation of the adult members at this meeting. "We've been worried sick. I'm going to bed." He patted Bob on the back and said, "She's all yours. It's not going to be easy."

My friends went upstairs, trying to be inconspicuous, and crashed in empty bedrooms. "We're glad you're home safe. We're going to spend the night," was their only comment.

I was angry, sleepy and bewildered. I was trying so hard to be a resigned grown-up about this whole matter yet here I was looking like a waif and being reprimanded by my son.

"We'll all talk in the morning," I yawned. I didn't want to think or feel or hear anything more today.

And in the morning Bob was still there. I vaguely remember being asked to marry him every time I rolled over, Bob vowing not to let me get to sleep until I said yes. Bob did confirm this fact in the morning or I may have excused it as a dream. It was not until I was fully awake that I snuggled up to him and said, "Yes, I think I should say, yes."

We were still chuckling with this memory when we reached the bottom of the slope. We are now both exhausted. We had been skiing since early morning and now it was four o'clock on Monday afternoon. Filly and Freddie will be married this Friday. The wedding is only days away. Only days away.

I am becoming a frequent flyer. I am racking up those miles. By the time Filly and Freddie are married, Bob and I will have earned us a very much-needed free trip somewhere, anywhere. And so, I am airborne again. The wedding is in only three days. When I fly back from Miami, this time, I will officially be a mother-in-law. I am tense, excited, exhausted and happy. I am trying to pretend yesterday did not exist, but it did, all twenty-four excruciating hours of it. Twenty-four hours loaded with errands and phone calls and yes, one more trip to the bank. (We're only $7,000 over budget. How lucky can you get!) It is a good thing Bob and I are rested and happy after our little excursion to Vermont. We had no idea what was awaiting us. If we had only known.

We walked into a spotless house with the phone ringing hysterically off the wall. "Where have you been?" screamed our lawyer. "Why didn't you leave a number where you could have been reached?"

"Where have you been?" wailed the realtor. "The owners of the house you bought are hysterical."

"Where have you been?" shouted the mortgage broker. "We've got just twenty-four hours to change one clause in the contract."

"Where have you been? Where have you been? Where have you been?"

Every phone call begins with the same lament. But it's cool. We're tanned and relaxed. No problem. It takes a while for reality and hysteria to close in. What do you mean twenty-four hours. We are leaving for Miami at nine o'clock Wednesday, that's all the time we have left. There is too much to do; too much to be resolved. No sooner do we put that instrument of reality back to rest in its cradle, than its incessant buzz begins again. The caterer is finally returning our call, confirming that the final figure is really $7,000 over what we had planned. A trip to the bank becomes another necessity. We are no longer real cool. A slow burn is beginning. Our tans have turned chalk white. There are too many things to accomplish in only twenty-four hours.

Bob and I take the phone off the hook and fall asleep exhausted with the list of to dos for Tuesday on our minds. Our sleep time seems to fly and soon we are gulping down coffee and splitting up the list of errands. He kindly takes the banking chore since I hate asking those sweet people at the bank for more money. And we are off and running.

After making time for my conference work at Sarah Lawrence (Did I fail to mention that through all this I am also going to school?), I raced back to Greenwich to pick up my gown for the wedding. The owner of the store had promised to deliver it to my eagerly awaiting hands at one o'clock promptly. I burst into the store with a carefully calculated timetable in my head. I would have just enough time to try on the dress and run to my next stop. My schedule was timed to perfection. My heart stopped dead and wound up somewhere on the floor when I spotted my dress neatly hung and painfully still pinned together with straight pins.

"I just wanted you to try it on one more time. I want it to be perfect." I obediently did as I was told and tried the dress on while I pictured my schedule floating out the window. I said the first of one of many little prayers I was to say today. The dress did look perfect but I would have been a whole lot happier if it had already been sewn.

"I'll be back at 5:30," I said lamely. "Please don't close the store before I get back," I pleaded.

"Of course not sweetheart; I'll even bring it to your house if you like."

And I knew she would. My dressmaker had become my newfound friend and confidante. She was my pal. I trusted her, but I still said another little prayer.

My manicure and another pedicure (I'm beginning to like them) came next. This time it was not relaxing. The salon was over booked and I was nervous and antsy thinking about all the things I had to do. I was running far behind schedule; so was the beauty salon. Bob managed to find me at this point in time. He looked frazzled. He had just received a phone call from the realtor.

"Don't worry about a thing," the realtor had soothingly begun, "But there's been a big mistake. The bulletin went out and it states your open house is today, Tuesday, instead of Thursday when you're gone. I couldn't reach the printer in time to change it once I realized the goof."

Well, Bob said the realtors had been coming to the house in packs and ringing the doorbell in droves. He couldn't even take a shower (alas this seems to be his fate) until he posted a big MISTAKE sign on the front door. It read, "MISTAKE . . . OPEN HOUSE THURSDAY MARCH 10." He finally managed to shower in peace with the front door securely double bolted shut and the phone once again off the hook.

His tuxedo experience was just as unsettling as my dress fiasco. The cuffs had to be redone at the last minute. "So what," I tried to assure him. "Will anyone know if one is slightly shorter than the other? What difference does it make? No one will notice." One look at his expression and I knew it mattered a lot. It made a lot of difference to him.

"And I guess no one will know that your dress is being held together with safety pins."

Boy are we getting testy. The day (which is not nearly over) is taking its toll. I suddenly decide to look at my watch. With alarm, I realize that I cannot wait for my toes to dry. Begging for possession of the foam rubber thongs upon my pretty pink feet, I plod out of the door a picture of exhausted, understated, nervous, unsophisticated, floppy confusion. I say another little prayer. This time it is a prayer that no one will see me. It is March and my toes are getting frostbitten. I have forgotten how far away I have parked my car. I'm on a desperate mission. I am off to get my dress and it is five minutes until closing. I try to park the car as close to the dress shop as possible but I am still left across the street. It is now 5:35 and rush hour on Main Street in Greenwich. I try to calmly lock my car holding my head up high and not looking at my feet. With foam rubber thongs on my feet, it is necessary to lift my legs up high with each step as if stepping over piles in order not to fall flat on my face. I pray twice as hard that no one I know will bear witness to this spectacle. Flip-flopping across the street with cotton between my toes, I am no longer mortified at my appearance. I just want my dress! Like a one-woman military coup, I had come to claim what was mine. I was rewarded. I was jubilant. It had no pins. The enemy had been conquered. It hung there, waiting for me to claim it. I wanted to hug the yards of peach silk; instead I hugged Susan. She came through. It was ready. "Mazel Tov," she shouted as I raced out the door.

"What's that you have on your feet?" she called out after me.

"Nothing Susan, I'll see you at Passover." I shouted as I made a little mental note. Passover is just two weeks away. Just two weeks after the wedding. Susan, my newfound dressmaker, is also my newfound friend and she'll celebrate the holiday with us. I love holidays and parties. My Seder this year happens to fall on Good Friday so I'll have to have some fish. Life keeps on getting more interesting. Ah diversity....

I return home to my barricaded house with the MISTAKE sign on the front door. I make a tall drink for Bob and one for myself as we try to settle down and relax. It is not meant to be. My son has already left for the airport. A phone call informs me that his flight has been canceled and rearranged by a well-meaning airline. He is now stranded at the wrong airport and steaming while he tries to book another flight. But not to worry Mom, it'll be all right. Several strong words flash through my brain. Realtors, lawyers, airlines; all have been assigned improper adjectives. Bob and I pour ourselves another drink. (This is very odd since neither of us drink very much.) We fall asleep exhausted and numb. Ah vodka....

I think it is time to put my pencil down. I really should try to get some sleep. The plane will be landing in less than an hour. The next few days promise to bring a whirlwind of activity. Filly and Freddie are the official greeters. They've said they will try to personally greet each flight of incoming relatives. (What enthusiasm!) I look over at Bob. He has not opened his eyes for the entire flight. I lean my head on his shoulder and finally fall asleep.

F my name is Filly. I'm gonna marry Freddie. We're gonna live in Florida and we'll sell futons. I woke up with this silly ditty spinning in my head. We had landed. I laughed at my own thoughts. That silly little song was not far from the truth. My heart leaps with joy and stops somewhere in my throat as I spot Filly and Robin, her maid of honor, waiting to greet us. It seems like only yesterday, they were clapping their hands and singing the song still playing in my head. Dressed in their shorts, with no make-up on, they look about twelve-years-old. This is my baby and her best friend since third grade. Time seems to suddenly stand still. It is hard to believe in two days Filly will be a married woman.

"Hi, Mz. V.," yells Robin. I am pulled back to reality. Filly's best friend looks so much like her they could pass for sisters and often do.

"Hi, Mommy, Hi Bob," yells Filly. "I'm getting married on Friday!"

There are hugs and tears and laughter; the entire airport now knows what the chaos is about. The two little girls in my mind's eye a moment ago, are now two grown women. In several days an important threshold will be crossed, but for now tears are quickly wiped away and I begin to sing out loud.

"F my name is Filly, etc. etc." Robin and Filly roar.

"Do you remember when we used to sing that song, Filler?" Robin asks between giggles.

"I sure do; do you remember when you cut off my pigtails, Robber?" Filly and Robin have reverted back to treasured old nicknames and memories.

"Oh my God Filler, wasn't that awful? I thought my mother was going to kill me. Remember she made me buy you a Barbie doll."

And so it went; talk so fast and reminiscent it resembled an old home movie shown at fast speed. As each girl from Filly's wedding party arrived, the scene was repeated. I am sure the same was going on with Freddie and his friends. All of a sudden, I remembered my dress! I had carried it on the plane, terrified of losing it in checked on luggage. (I had already lost a piece of luggage on one of my other trips to Miami and it took five days to find me. I didn't have five days to spare now.)

"Where is my dress?" I looked around with a look of frantic panic.

"Right here, Mz. V., you gave it to me as soon as you got off the plane." Robin is still laughing. "Remember?"

I don't remember, but that's OK. Everything is happening so fast. It's off to our hotel. So far so good. Our accommodations are everything we wanted, a spacious suite overlooking the ocean. It is soon filled with six bridesmaid's gowns and a fairytale bridal gown and veil. I begin to get weepy looking at the empty dress but too much is going on to take the time for sentiment. I still cannot truly believe in two days my Filly will really walk down the aisle dressed like Cinderella. All of a sudden I remember my own dress again. "Where is my dress?" I ask beseechingly of anyone within earshot.

"Right here." It is Bob who answers this time. My dress seems to be the one thing I cannot keep track of, it keeps disappearing. Bob and Robin are now laughing it up at my expense but it's OK, I deserve to be a little bit jittery.

"It's OK, Mz. V. We'll take care of it. We're in control." And they were.

I decide to take a walk next door to see how my son, Joe, is settling in. One quick look tells me fine, just fine. Tuxedos are strewn everywhere amidst sneakers, bathing suits and towels. The room resembles a boys' dormitory already and they've been in there less than twenty-four hours. Our decision to have many close but separate rooms is a wise one. All systems seem ready to go. We are off and running to Filly and Freddie's house.

It is Wednesday evening. The kids (Filly and Freddie will probably always be kids in my heart) are having everyone over to their house for a barbeque. I take a few more deep breaths (I am really getting good at deep breathing exercises) and we set out for their party. I am worried about everything but all my worries seem to vanish into the tropical air. There is a joy in the shimmering moonlight and it seems to be contagious. My in-laws (my first husband's parents) meet Bob for the first time and actually appear to like him. Why I find this a surprise is beyond me. I love him, after all. My heart tells me how hard this must be for them. It's like meeting a replacement for something that is irreplaceable. No parent should ever lose a child. Losing their only child and meeting and greeting the man who will marry his bride and be the stepfather of his children must be especially straining. I hug them a little longer and I love them especially more. I wipe away my tears, again.

I go through Wednesday evening as if in a strange kind of never-never land. I am in some unusual and foreign middle earth. I'm happy, happier than I can ever remember, but, I'm uncertain and walking in uncharted territory. For a moment my mind lingers on my first husband. How happy and proud he would have been to see this moment. I shake myself back to reality. It was not to be and I have promised myself not to play that game.

"Hi, Mommy." It is Filly and Freddie snapping me back to the present moment. "Can you believe it? We're getting married on Friday." They are radiant and smiling. My melancholy daydreams vanish and I am once again engulfed in their happiness. Robin starts to sing. "R my name is Robin, I'm gonna marry Ronnie," etc. etc. Everyone takes a turn and a beer and joins in the song from the girls' childhood. It is soon my turn.

"D my name is Diana, I'm gonna marry . . . oh no, it doesn't work. Bob your name doesn't start with a D. It's no good. We can't get married. I've got to find a David or a Donald." The moment is absolutely silly and filled with giggles but I have a curious lump in my stomach. "Or you'll have to find a Rosalie or a Barbara depending on if you're Robert or Bob, and we don't make dresses. Oh heavens, where did I leave my dress?" I've become very serious or delirious, I'm not sure which.

"Mz. V., Bob and I put it away. You're just being a nervous Mom, relax. It's OK if Bob's name doesn't start with a D." Although Robin is laughing, I am listening seriously.

"Stop. Stop." Bob has the floor now. "I have a solution."

"Both of you will change your names!" shouts Robin.

"No, Robber, Diana will have to call me Doc." Bob is quick to the rescue as usual sensing my change of mood and trying to joke me out of it. My wheels start to turn.

"What a great idea. That's wonderful. D my name is Diana, I'm gonna marry Doc. We'll live in Darien and practice dentistry and I will find my dress. Yeh, it works!"

There is more laughter and more silliness all evening. I am much calmer. For some odd reason I am really quite glad the rhyme worked out. The evening is now breaking up. There is still all day Thursday left before the momentous heralding of Friday, March 11. I am sure the day will disappear in a blur of emotions and activity. We are off to a very good start. I survey all the empty beer cans around me and hope the headaches will not be too bad tomorrow. Tomorrow. The rehearsal dinner. I hear that Freddie's Dad has been cooking for days with his friends. It should be some feast.

Back at our hotel, I ask Bob one more time, exactly where he has put my dress. He tells me assuringly it is hanging right next to his tuxedo. Snuggling up into his arms, I look up at his smiling face. "What's up Doc?" I ask secure and in love. As always Bob rises to the occasion. Ah bliss....

"Hi Mommy." My daughter's voice wakes me from a surprisingly peaceful slumber. "It's pouring out, what are we going to do?" There is panic in her voice. "Fred's Dad has planned the whole rehearsal dinner outside and everyone wanted to spend the day at the beach. What are we going to do?"

"A rain dance, to try and stop it maybe?" I am trying to be funny. I wait for the laughter at the other end of the phone. There is none. I sense the tension brewing with the clouds. I pull myself out of bed, kiss Doc, and draw back the curtains. Sure enough it is wet, gray, windy and cold out there. The beach is deserted. The bridal party will have to put their tans on hold. I rush back to the phone trying to think of some reassuring words for Filly.

"It's only eight o'clock in the morning sweetheart. Maybe it will clear up." If I sounded less than confidant, it was because the morning news was showing one big cloud cover over the entire state of Florida. This television weatherman was not helping.

"Mom, you don't sound so sure. Please don't let it rain."

"OK, Filly, I'll do whatever is in my power to make it stop." I was starting to sound like a voodoo priestess, but at least it broke the tension and Filly began to laugh. With another kiss of encouragement through the receiver, I hung up the phone and quickly started a litany of special little prayers. "Dear God, please give us a sunny day tomorrow," was high on my list of requests. It was time to start hopping and hoping. Rain or shine there were millions of things to get done today. We had a wedding tomorrow. My things to do list had grown dramatically since we'd arrived. There was no time to waste.

Running around in the rain all morning must have been taken as a sacrificial offering, because somewhere around noon the sun broke through the clouds. A delighted bridal party and an assortment of various guests poured out onto the beach. The sun and the surf guaranteed self-entertainment. I began to wonder secretly if Fred's Dad had done his share of praying this morning and to whom. Do Jews and Buddhists have patron saints? Is there a patron saint for the father of the groom or for the mother of the bride, or for belly dancers? I guessed it really didn't matter. I was sure all the prayers were falling on one God's ears. Boy he must have been overwhelmed. It really didn't matter at all. All the prayers were answered, in mass. The day became one beyond compare. By the time we were off to church for the rehearsal, everyone was light, carefree and slightly sunburned.

Now, I must say, I've grown to love Miami, I really have, but as we walked into the church we had our geographic location written clearly all over us. It stated, Fairfield County, CT. We stood out like pink and green peacocks. Bob in his double-breasted gray Armani suit could have fit in anywhere but Joe and I were dead giveaways, creatures from another planet. While all the other ushers, Freddie's friends and relatives from Miami, stood at the alter dressed in basic Don Johnson black and white, shirts open to the navel with several gold chains around their necks and wrists, my son stood there in his pink and green sport jacket, white buttoned down shirt, pink tie, green pants and docksiders with no socks. I was sure he was wearing his Nantucket whale belt as well, but from where I was standing I couldn't tell. Joe had donned every piece of Preppie clothing he owned to achieve the desired affect, his sister's smile and laughter. Never, as a mother, have I been prouder of having raised two really different and special kids, their differences strikingly apparent in their comparative geographical dress. Ah the good ole USA....

The church rehearsal, itself, became one big happy reunion. It was a gathering of family and friends who had shared many sad events in the past, all ready to celebrate a joyous occasion; all ready to party and treasure every moment. Our parish priest from Darien flew down to Miami to marry his longtime youth group member to the man of her dreams. He was also caught up in the reunion of many of Filly's friends and the planning of more happy times. There would be more weddings in store for him this summer. "There is a time for every purpose under heaven," so the saying goes, and for this group of "kids" the time was for weddings.

A caravan of cars make their way from the church to Freddie's Dad's house. We have all been lost in Miami several times already and go to great lengths not to lose sight of the car in front of us. We travel like a swarm of bees, swooping into Marakesh, drawn to honey. The smell of the Arabic cooking permeates the air for blocks surrounding the house. My incoming swarm is hugged and kissed and coddled and caressed by Freddie's family. I feel like a queen bee arriving with her hive. The hives quickly mingle amidst the exotic aromas, mixtures of accents and the sound of the seductive Arabic instruments. The night is splendid. I give the rehearsal dinner ten stars.

The belly dancers completed the balmy evening with wild applause from all and introductory lessons for everyone. Freddie's Dad is beaming with glory as he dances with his son. I look around to see everyone enjoying themselves; the hives have truly mingled. Farkouk was teaching me rudimentary belly dancing; Bob was dancing to a light Latin beat with Carolina and even Grandpa was moving his hips to boogie, or is that belly with one of the belly dancers. Grandma, not to be outdone, quickly asked for a cha-cha, which took on a Casablanca flair when played on the Arabic instruments. No belly dancer was going to steal her man. They danced the night away. Even Father A clapped and stomped and roared with laughter. It was, he said, like no other rehearsal dinner he had ever attended. Then again, we are like few other families in our ethnic diversity.

Father A was a wonderful sport, especially later on in the evening when a pretty blonde friend of the family, who had had too much to drink, started pouring out her confession, in Spanish. I am not sure he understood a word but he appeared kind and compassionate as she cried on through gin-stained tears.

I suppose as a young good looking Irish Catholic priest he must be used to this scene. "What woman wouldn't want to confess all her sins to him?" laughed one of my girlfriends, "And maybe invent a few too." The line for confessions was starting to grow with my friend next in line, when Father A graciously made an exit. I'm sure he said a few Hail Marys all the way home. I know I did. Prayers of thanks and prayers of hope seem always to be on my lips.

Tomorrow is ecumenical wedding, a phrase coined by someone at the party. The evening's interesting mix of people are getting tired and the day is coming to an end. I note with pride all the people I love, Jews, Christians, Mexicans, Buddhists, Cubans, Italians, you name it and they are all here. All of them, in one way or another, play a very special part in my life. We leave the party singing, "What a Wonderful World." Louis Armstrong we are not, but there is a special feeling in the air. I tell this to Bob. "That's because you're a very special lady," he whispers to me. God, I love this guy. Tomorrow is a big day and we decide it's time to get some sleep. Ah what a wonderful world....

Louis Armstrong is still crooning to me, or is it Bob, when I open my eyes. Ah what a wonderful world it is! A little hesitantly, I pull back the curtains and the sun comes pouring in. I literally jump with joy. "Yahoo! Look at the day!" I scream to Bob. You must really know and love Miami to appreciate what the weatherman and God had in store for us today. The day was kissed with perfection. There is no humidity; there are no clouds in the sky; just bright blue heavens as far as you can see. The beach is already filling up and it is only eight o'clock in the morning. With a big sigh of relief, and one more look at the dazzling day, I whisper a little prayer of thanks and go to answer the phone.

"Hi, Mommy, I'm getting married today. Are you psyched or what?" It's my baby calling and yes, I am psyched. (Our family phrase for very excited.)

"Hi Filly, I sure am and I even got a fantastic night's sleep. Freddie's Dad really put on quite a party last night. I still can't believe how really well everyone got along. What's the first thing on the agenda today?"

"Hair and then make-up. I'll meet you at the Salon at eleven. Bye now, I've got to run. Love Ya." Filly is off and running. Bob is still in bed.

Eleven o'clock is still ringing rather harshly in my ears. The wedding is a candlelight service in church and will not begin till seven o'clock. Visions of bedraggled bridesmaids and an exhausted mother of the bride loom before my eyes, but my fears are all for naught. My entourage of light in the loafer male friends will see to it that everyone remains looking fresh and radiant. They have all been patiently awaiting this day, ready to help us become the glamorous women they wish they were.

Now I should pause here a moment to explain another illustrious circle of friends. For some inexplicable rational reason, many of my best friends are gay men. A channeler (a person who talks to you through spirit guides) once told me that this is because I once was a Greek warrior, beloved by many of my men (yes I was a man in that lifetime). The men beneath me (no joke intended) promised to follow me with service into eternity. If these were in fact my long lost troops, they followed me once again into battle, this time armed with scissors, hair spray, eye make-up and blush, eager to wait on us hand and foot.

Bob took a while to adjust to this particular group of my friends. Both sides approached each other with caution. Bob left me on many occasions, dangling pink plastic monkeys in my frozen margaritas while discussing past life experiences with my friends in various Greenwich Village Mexican restaurants. But he has grown to like them (well not in the way he likes me). He would want me to make that point clear. He still shudders when he thinks of the first time I took him to Fire Island.

"Do not leave my side for a moment," he pleaded. Maybe I had introduced my friends too soon. Maybe he wasn't ready for tea dancing on the island. He still cannot fully understand why I listened intently to a man tell me how to use my hair to become more of a woman. This particular fellow had demonstrated very encouragingly with a long blonde wig. Bob and I have much more to learn about each other. It will be exciting. I've been told this is not our first lifetime together, but on with the wedding.

With my troops gathered around me, the frazzled women turned into a bevy of beauties. Hair gleamed, eyes sparkled, and make-up is set and what? You want me to put Vaseline on my teeth! Why?

"So your teeth will look whiter and shiny in the photos sweetie and the lipstick won't run. Take my word for it Dearie. Believe me!"

And we did. And it worked. Four hours later we emerged as close to perfection as was possible. We walked out into the solid sunshine of reality and wind and parking tickets on all of our cars. Our entourage of beauty keepers promised to follow us faithfully throughout the day with touch up accessories in hand. We panicked momentarily, when it appeared my sister Ali was lost. She had left the Salon an hour ago on a quest for crazy glue to repair a broken earring. She finally arrived back at the Salon, as we were all leaving. She was frustrated at the dilemma she had found herself in. My sister, who had studied French, could not speak a word of Spanish. For the first time, my years of Spanish were more of an advantage. Aha! This was Miami. She could not find a store anywhere within a mile radius where someone could speak English, never mind French. Ah yes, little sister, you are in Miami. I will say no more.

Filly hopped into the car with me. "Mom that's your third parking ticket in three days. They're really strict down here. You've got to put money in the meter."

"That's the last thing on my mind Filly. By now we're supporting the Dade County meter violation patrol. With all of our tickets combined they could take a week's vacation in Cuba. Besides, I can't write a check to a parking meter." My change purse, weighted down with quarters had been exhausted days ago.

"Oh Mom, you're so silly. I can't believe I'm getting married today. I thought I'd be a nervous wreck today but I even slept real well last night. I had a wild dream though. Actually it was rather uplifting. Grandpa Jack showed up at Viscaya for the wedding and it wasn't like he was a ghost. He wasn't dead, or anything. He had just aged. He wasn't the young Grandpa I remembered. He was old and walked with a cane. No one was even surprised to see him. He hugged me and kissed me, and I introduced him to Freddie. He told me he had to leave ten years ago when he did because he knew we would all be suffering through many ordeals and he just couldn't bear to witness them first-hand. It was his choice to go. He put his arm around me and whispered in my ear that everything was going to be fine and he would always be around if I needed him. Mom are you OK? I shouldn't have told you my dream. Don't cry! Remember you promised."

"No, it's OK Filly, they're happy tears. I think it was a good dream and I think it was real and I'm not at all upset. I wouldn't dare cry and let all this mascara run. I would look like a raccoon. I can't believe we've got only one hour left to get dressed before the photographer arrives. We better step on it."

And step on it I did, the accelerator that is, and received a new type of Dade County ticket. This one was for speeding. I wondered out loud if the officer's time wouldn't have been better spent chasing drug dealers like on Miami Vice. I should have kept my thoughts to myself. I could feel his stony glaze coming out from behind his mirrored sunglasses. I could also see my own reflection in them. My perfectly coifed hair was blowing in the wind and getting messed. Filly told me to stop and be quiet, while my mouth was opening in more protest. I decided to take her advice and we very slowly headed back to the hotel, ticket in hand. Doing the speed limit across the causeway, cars passed us left and right honking and cursing. Ah law and order....

We arrived back at the room one half hour after the photographer. Bob, my darling, had carefully planned ahead and had wine, beer, and lots of edibles on hand. He knew we would not be thinking of food unless it was placed right in front of us. This he did. The photographer and his wife were fed and comfortable and not at all in a hurry until they looked at their watches. They then told us we had better move it. Hurry! They wanted to catch the sunset at Viscaya. Foamy clouds were drifting in and it promised to be a photographer's dream. Perfect conditions for a perfect sunset. It would certainly help if he had the whole bridal party for the picture so would we please hurry. Bob stood there calmly in a dripping wet bathing suit. It was a good thing he was calm. Everyone around him went into a sudden tailspin of hysteria. Robin, Filly's maid of honor, did justice to her title. Remaining calm as well, she began to look at the display of six bras Filly had brought to try on with her gown. I went into a state of catatonic shock. Ali poured everyone a drink and said something appropriate, (or not) in French. I couldn't tell.

"This one is perfect. It's comfortable and I can move in it. This is the bra I'll wear." Filly was very relieved with the fact one of the bras worked. I was still adrift in never-never land looking for my own dress.

"I don't think so Filly," giggled Robin. Ali and I looked on in perplexed shock. The back of the bra stretched across Filly's bare back and her gown was on. Ali jumped to the rescue. We have a fashion consultant in the family for a very good reason.

"No Filly," Ali said calmly. "This is the bra you should wear."

"I can't Ali, my boobs hang out." Filly looked like she was near tears and still the photographer kept shooting.

"Yes you can. No one is going to be looking at your boobs. Here let me sew the bra right into place like so." Ali was being so maternal. This was a new side of her I was seeing and boy was I grateful.

"That's perfect, Ali. Please hurry!" Filly was getting anxious. "That's perfect Ali. Please hurry!" The photographer was also getting anxious as he clicked away. The wedding album had begun.

Drifting around in shock, I chose this time to go and check on the boys next door. I brought a six-pack of beer with me. It was a ridiculous offering. Some of their pictures had already been taken amidst cases of empty and full cans and bottles of beer. An assortment of very confused young men was running around trying to figure out the rituals of tuxedo dressing. My son-in-law to almost be, kissed my cheek, took the beer (you could always use another six I guess) and told me I looked beautiful but nervous and confused, and escorted me to the door.

Back in the secure chaos of the women's chambers, I was glad to see Filly almost all sewn in. The girls were all dressed and Bob was halfway into his tux. The photographer was still clicking as we kept dressing.

"Call the family and have all the close relatives meet us at church for the family photos," the photographer screamed back to me as we were all finally leaving the hotel. I race back up to the room in high heels and a gown as fast as is possible in that attire and make all the required phone calls. Bob and Robin are left in charge of Filly and are doing a far better job than I could ever do today in keeping her calm. It is now five o'clock and everyone I call says they have already been informed they must be at the church by six o'clock. But it is now already five o'clock and we will need a huge miracle to get to the church by six. Racing back down the stairs I make myself another promise not to cry. I have already almost broken that promise on several occasions during the dress up session. Twice to be exact. The first time was when Bob placed the pearls he had bought Filly around her neck. It was heart-stopping time. The second was when Robin kissed Filly and said, "I love you Filler, you look beautiful, just like a princess."

I wait impatiently for the elevator to take me back down to the lobby. It seems to take an eternity. As it finally reaches my floor and I go to step on, Freddie and Joe race off with panic on their faces.

"What's wrong?" I manage to squeak with a voice I do not even recognize. I also begin to feel faint.

144

"Cash, the damn limousine drivers want to be paid in cash. But don't worry Mom. All the guys are pooling their resources and we're getting close."

Close, close, cash, how could seven guys come up with $1,200 cash? "That's ridiculous," I had somehow found my voice. "We have a certified check for them and that's as good as cash." Not only had I found my voice, it was rising and I was ready to storm troop the situation.

"Mom," (Freddie had called me mom!) "You don't understand. This is Miami. They really want cash."

Properly chastised, I sealed my lips all the way down to the lobby. Of course there was no one in the elevator to complain to. I found Bob talking patiently to a group of limo drivers that looked as if they all had starring roles in the Godfather. I also found one hysterical looking bride being calmed by her best friend and aunt and being kept a safe distance away from the turmoil. My lips became unsealed and I was ready to invade the discussion. I am after all the mother of the bride and will not see anyone upset Filly. I see Bob waving his hand up and down for me to back off and cool down. Shush, his hand kept saying. It's all under control. And I guess it finally was, but they still refused to take our check. By cashing a check at the front desk and emptying everyone's cash reserve, we were finally on our way.

In the limousine, I sit with my sister Ali across from Filly. She is safely snuggled between Robin and Bob. To make up for the aggravation they have caused us, the limo drivers were told to keep the champagne flowing. Filly seems uncannily relaxed.

"Hi, Mommy! I'm getting married in less than two hours. Can you believe it? Are you psyched?" How was she remaining so calm? It must be the champagne. Psychotic was more the word for my state of mind right now. I smiled and told Filly how truly beautiful she looked, and she did, but my mind was on the church. It was now six o'clock and we were not headed there to take pictures with all the grandmothers. We were on our way to catch the sunset. It had better be a beauty; the photographers will not have to explain to all the grandparents where we were; I will. The photographers are lucky.

The photographs of the bridal party, taken at Viscaya with the sun setting in the background, are dramatic. So will my mother be when she finally sees me. It is now seven o'clock; we have not yet left for the church. We are still taking pictures. The florist manages to track me down. I had promised to pay the remainder of his bill at six o'clock in front of the church. Thankfully he accepts a check. (God only knows where we would have gotten more cash?)

I ask him meekly how everything is going in church. Filly should have been walking down the aisle about now. We are running very late.

"Oh fine," he smiles pocketing his check. "People are just beginning to arrive. Nothing in Miami ever starts on time, but, there are a bunch of people who've been hanging around from around say, six o'clock. They must be from out of town. They really looked upset when the rest of the guests started to arrive. They kept talking about family photos or something." With this little soliloquy, and a few last minute instructions on whose flowers were whose, he departed. My heart was sinking as fast as my bank account and the sun when I thought of all the wandering assortment of relatives waiting to be captured on film, but one look at Filly and Freddie and I realized these were the only two people who mattered today. With Freddie's arm around Filly's waist, the photographer shot the last remaining photos of the couple before the wedding. They were relaxed and serene as the sun gave a panoramic backdrop to their kisses and slid majestically into Biscayne Bay.

"Ali, how are my boobs?" We are back in the limo and finally on our way to the church. "Are you sure Ali? How can you tell? It's dark out. And Mom stop being nervous or I'll be nervous. I can tell you're nervous." Her serenity has cracked.

"Filly, it's dark outside. I am not nervous now. (Thank heavens we are taking turns.) You can't even see my face. Relax." I have said the wrong thing.

"If you can't even see my face, how can Ali see my boobs? Did she bring her needle and thread?" Filly sounds as if she is panicking.

And Ali did have the needle, threaded and ready. In fact she followed Filly around with it for the first half of the evening just as she had promised. Poor Filly, separated from her honey once again, had lost the tranquility so evident at the photo sessions. Even the photographer had remarked he had never seen a calmer bride. Now she appeared to be going into catatonic shock. She stopped babbling and didn't say a word for what seemed like an eternity. Until we finally pulled up to the church. At 7:45. Only forty-five minutes late. Not so bad by Miami standards, I am told.

"What are all these people doing here?" Filly looks as white as her gown and I am afraid she will faint. "I'm not getting out of the limo!"

Oh no, Dr. Spock didn't cover this problem in his parenting books. He left me dangling somewhere when Filly was about twelve years old. I tried to think of the most logical explanation for all the people at the church and then decided to tell Filly the absolute truth. It always seemed to work the best although now it seemed rather silly.

"They are here because you invited them Filly, remember? You're getting married today." I assume I said the right thing because all she uttered was a very quiet, "Oh." Then, "Where is Grandpa? I don't see Grandpa!"

I did. He was racing frantically toward our limo. Our job of keeping Filly calm would soon be over. She would be all his. He would have to take over from here.

Filly grabbed my arm as I tried to exit the limo. She was regaining her composure. "Mom, please don't cry and make sure everyone gets the right flowers." My super organizer was back to her old self.

Well I tried to fulfill my promises and didn't do too badly. I managed to distribute the variety of corsages and lapel roses while pacifying the throngs of relatives who had been waiting to have their family photos taken, and become recorded for posterity. At 7:55 with only one leftover boutonniere, I begged everyone lingering around to please be seated. I feared if they did not, Filly's Grandpa would never be able to persuade her to leave the car.

With one long glance up the aisle before I was seated, I knew we were in trouble. The seats reserved for Grandpa and Grandma were taken. Bob jumped in to the rescue and rearranged the first three rows accordingly to the warm up tune of the organ. Everyone was congenial but Grandma was elated. In her eyes Bob had just been elevated to sainthood. The first Jewish patron saint in charge of wedding seating arrangements. He rushed back down to my side and to the strains of "Ave Maria," I walked down the aisle clutching my son's arm on one side and Bob's on the other.

My promise not to cry would have been obliterated at this moment, hearing the sound of my much-loved hymn, but I bit my lip so hard, it bled. Memories of May crownings of the Blessed Virgin Mary filled my mind with lilacs. It was the thought of lilacs that brought me back to reality. I paid attention to the flower arrangements lining the aisle. They were as beautiful as the florist had promised. I stopped biting my lip and looked up and smiled. What were all these people doing here? The church was packed, and looking at the love on everyone's faces brought a glow to my spirit that put me at one with the candlelit church. As Bob and I took our place in the front pew and my son walked up to his spot on the altar, the sound of "Eres Tu" began. My mother began to cry hysterically two chords into the music and it wasn't even "Here Comes the Bride." Maybe that was why? The kids had chosen their favorite Spanish love song. For a brief moment, I thought this might be the reason she was crying, another smack in the face of tradition, but it wasn't. Her eyes were glued on her baby granddaughter, smiling radiantly on her grandfather's arm. I looked up bravely and instantly noticed not my daughter but Grandpa's lapel. He was walking down the aisle without a boutonniere. That explained the extra one. Grandpa, tucked in the limo with Filly, had escaped my count. My mother-in-law, as well, began to cry openly and I prayed it was not because of the missing boutonniere. With all the tears around me, I began to realize that fulfilling my promise would require my Greek warrior image. I tried to stand proud and tall. It worked. As Filly stopped next to me to leave her Grandpa's side, all the tears welling up inside me pumped me up to feeling about ten feet tall. As she kissed me on the cheek and left to join her husband, I felt as proud as a peacock and as humble as a lamb. I had so much to be thankful for. I closed my eyes for a moment, swallowed back more restrained tears, said a little prayer and hoped that somehow, someway, her Daddy and mine had witnessed this day.

I looked up with glazed eyes and smiled at the four little flower girls. They all looked like little princess brides; white babies breath in their hair and white eyelet dresses trimmed in blue ribbons. They sat on the steps of the altar and looked adoringly up at their beloved Filly. It seemed like yesterday that Filly and her friends were that young.

I courageously looked up at the altar and saw Robin, composed and self-assured. I thought back to the days, years ago, when she took Filly skiing for the first time. My mind became a video of old memories as I looked upon each bridesmaid. I saw Bonnie dancing on stage with Filly in their years together in the dance troupe. I saw Alex singing songs from Godspell, during their years in youth group. I saw Priscilla being everyone's best friend and confidant. The years of their childhoods danced in my mind in flighty images of proms, birthday parties, and sleepovers. I looked over to the ushers and saw my son valiantly wiping away tears that he had made no promise to control. At this point I almost broke what was now beginning to seem like a silly promise. I reached for a Kleenex and dabbed at my eyes. The thought of my face streaked with all the precisely placed cosmetics brought my tears to a standstill and actually caused me to giggle. Even though both grandmothers were still crying right behind me, I began to believe that I could actually fulfill this promise.

Two things had actually happened to help hold back the impending tears. My stomach began to growl, loudly; I realized I was starving. It was now almost 8:30 and I could not remember eating anything at all today. The other event was that my one-and-a-half-year-old niece finally realized that something was going on at the altar and kept calling for Ali. She obviously thought it was my younger sister Ali getting married. She and Filly do look a lot alike. She brought laughter and giggles from the crowd around her and was very confused when they pointed Ali out to her. Ali was sitting several pews behind everyone. I felt Ali should have been up in the first pew with us, but she had loyally stayed with Filly, ever ready with her needle and thread, until the very end. As the crowd in church, all hopeful partygoers, broke into a round of applause when Filly and Freddie were pronounced man and wife, I realized everyone must be as hungry as I was.

In pairs, this time, following the newlyweds, we filed out of the church. My mom took Bob's arm and her tears were drying; in fact she was beaming. I felt an overwhelming relief; the hard part was over. We were all going to have one hell of a party. And we did!

Now if the ceremony itself seemed to have lasted a lifetime of memories, the reception seemed like a fleeting moment. The hours between nine and one that required months of planning seemed to disappear into a sweet vapor of pleasant memories. I remember the grand entrance to Viscaya with all the guests being heralded by troubadours, dressed in period costumes and the torchbearers lighting the path for the royal couple. I was again lost in time and space. Bob was my Lord and I was his Lady presiding over this immense banquet. The weather continued to cooperate and the moon over Miami was full and benevolent. The breeze blew in over the bay and the palm trees swayed to the melodies played by the band.

Viscaya personnel had suggested that we keep the Gondola running all evening and we did with huge success. All evening the guests kept the Gondolier busy. Whenever Filly and Fred wanted to get away from the crowd of well wishers (as well as the ever-present photographer) they ran to the boat. Bobbing gently in the bay, viewing the big old mansion all aglow, listening to the music float over the water, you couldn't help but be lost somewhere in time. The world seemed to stand still. One particular cruise out, Bob and I and Ali went along with Filly and Freddie. The evening was drawing to a close and we stayed out for a while drifting out on the bay. The lapping of the waves against the side of the boat lulled my sister to sleep. It was a peaceful reflective time.

Filly and I congratulated each other and our men on a job well done. We laughed at some of the scenes at the party. Already they were becoming precious memories: Stu chasing his four-year-old daughter across the dance floor while never missing a Salsa beat; my sister Jackie doing the Samba with our ex-priest cousin; another cousin dancing to the Latin beat with a rose between his teeth; and my son Joe, caught up in the romantic atmosphere, taking long walks in the dusky gardens with a very good friend. Romance seemed to be in the air. I wondered out loud if she would still be his buddy when they returned home or if a magic spell had been cast on this relationship tonight. For there was a spell. This evening was as purely magical as we could have ever hoped for.

Our spell was quickly broken when we pulled up to the dock. My sister, now abruptly awakened from her dreams, stood up on the bow of the boat in her black evening gown and reached for a non-existent docking rope. She must have been sailing in her daydreams (she later told us this was indeed the case) and jumped up to help pull the boat in. On doing so, she nearly toppled overboard. The Gondolier caught his breath and my sister at the same time. It would have been quite the grand finale. Other guests, who were waiting for the boat to return and a turn at the cruise, were dancing at the water's edge. I was whisked into the arms of a dancing Latin waiter who finally returned me to the dock with my daughter and sister. We were all laughing with exhaustion. These two moments, captured on film, close my book of memories and a chapter in my life. Ah weddings....

I am in the air once again, being reflective. I am now on my way to New Orleans for a convention. Bob is once again sleeping soundly by my side. We have spent the last three days packing; packing for a three-day trip to New Orleans; packing for a lifetime as well. We will be moving into our new home in less than three weeks. Everything I own right now seems to be in a box. Life in a box.

The mailman added two more boxes yesterday to our ever-growing piles. They came from Mr. and Mrs. Fred Battah. It is over one month now since my daughter has become Mrs. Fred Battah. My heart takes a momentary nostalgic dip into a very empty spot. I suddenly miss Filly and Freddie and Miami very much. But we are all settling down into new realities of living, loving and learning. The Fairy Tale wedding is a dazzling memory etched in our hearts with a solid gold sunset.

I decide to open the smaller box first. I am glad Ali and Bob are standing right there. It contains the proofs of the wedding photos and we cannot devour them fast enough. The first two photos are of Filly dressing. One shows Ali sewing her into her gown and one shows Bob placing Filly's pearls around her neck. They are a few of the ones I recall the photographer taking. So are the last two. My tango with a waiter, and Filly and Ali and I sitting exhausted on the dock. Every other photo in between is a surprise and a delight. Where did the evening disappear? Thankfully into a photographer's proof book.

Inside the smaller box is also a videotape of the wedding. We are happier and more excited than three little mouseketeers on their way to see Mickey. We trip over each other in our race to the den. With a glass of wine in hand, we toast each other, point the remote control and press play. Within moments, every tear I had not shed during the ceremony comes pouring out of my eyes in torrents. With the first note of "Ave Maria," my sister and I start to cry and do not stop till we witness, for the second time, Filly and Freddie cutting their wedding cake. Even my calm levelheaded Bob, under the guise of handing us tissues, is dabbing at his own eyes. My baby is really married. The wonder of video has brought the reality home.

I know, before opening it, what is in the larger box. I still open it with the awe and the wonder of a mother viewing her first newborn. Indeed, the sights and smells of the pink blanket I had wrapped my precious firstborn daughter in, are very much in my mind. I lift the cover off the gold box while holding my breath and raise the protective tissue. My hand lovingly caresses the neatly folded silk gown, no longer personified by my princess, yet forever holding her image. I go back to my deep breathing lessons I have become so dependent upon in the weeks leading up to the wedding. I now make no effort whatsoever to hold back the tears. I want to quell the sudden ache. With Ali and Bob hugging me, and not saying a word, I replace the tissue and put the cover back on the gold box. I will put this box in a special place. This box the movers will not touch. Bob and I will take it ourselves to our new home. There it will become our first and most precious attic treasure.

The Beginning

## About the Author

Dianalee Velie lives and writes in Newbury, New Hampshire. She is a graduate of Sarah Lawrence College, and has a Master of Arts in Writing from Manhattanville College, where she has served as faculty advisor of *Inkwell: A Literary Magazine*. She has taught poetry, memoir and short story at universities and colleges in New York, Connecticut and New Hampshire, and in private workshops throughout the United States and Europe. Her award-winning poetry and short stories have been published in hundreds of literary journals throughout the USA and Canada. She enjoys traveling to rural school systems in Vermont and New Hampshire teaching poetry for the Children's Literacy Foundation. Her play, *Mama Says*, was directed by Daniel Quinn in a staged reading in New York City. He will also be producing her one–act play, *Womankind*, in the near future. She is the author of three books of poetry, *Glass House*, *First Edition*, and *The Many Roads to Paradise* published by Rock Village Publishing in Middleborough, Massachusetts, and has completed her fourth collection of poetry, *The Alchemy of Desire*. She is a long time member of the National League of American Pen Women. More details on her workshops and teaching schedule can be found on her website, dianaleevelie.com.

Dianalee was the Chairperson of the non-profit Velie Memorial Fund established to build the wonderful children's playground that now exists in Newbury, NH to honor the memory of her daughter-in-law, Currie-Hill Velie and her two grandsons, Joseph John Velie IV and Jack Jasper Velie.

Photo by Jason Baden

Dianalee Velie

## About the Artist

British artist Melinda Camber Porter (1953-2008) was known both as a writer and a painter. A solo traveling exhibition celebrating her oils on canvas and works on paper, curated by the late Leo Castelli, opened at the French Embassy in New York City in 1993. This exhibition traveled to fourteen major cities across the United States through 1997, making a special tour of museums in the western United States to coincide with the publication of her novel *Badlands*.

A film documenting the creation of the paintings featured in this solo exhibition entitled *The Art of Love*, shows regularly on Public Television stations nationally. Camber Porter's paintings have also served as the primary inspiration and as backdrops for several of her theatrical works. She created the backdrops, book, and lyrics for the musical *Night Angel*, which was originally performed at Lincoln Center in New York City, and the comedy *Boat Child*, which was performed at the Denver Center for the Performing Arts. She created the book, lyrics, and backdrops for the rock-opera-in-progress, *Journey to Benares*, with music, direction and choreography by Elizabeth Swados, which was performed at the Asia Society and Museum in New York City in November 2003.

From 1995 to 1997 Camber Porter completed *Luminous Bodies*, over three hundred fifty watercolors and pen and ink drawings. Between 1997 and 1998 she completed a major painting series, *Barcelona Point*, of sixteen large oils on canvas. A short film documenting the creating of the *Luminous Bodies* and *Barcelona Point* series, entitled *Luminous Journey*, is currently airing on Public Television. A feature documentary entitled *Sacred Journey*, which explores the influence of Native American culture and spirituality on the artist's visual works and her collaboration with Mi'kmaq musician Hubert Francis, is currently airing nationwide in Canada on the Aboriginal Peoples Television Network and on Vision Television.